Signs of Life

Gift
of
The Arizona
Daily Star

Other books by
JEAN FERRIS

Amen, Moses Gardenia

The Stainless Steel Rule

Invincible Summer

Looking for Home

Across the Grain

Relative Strangers

JEAN FERRIS

Signs of Life

FARRAR · STRAUS · GIROUX

NEW YORK

Copyright © 1995 by Jean Ferris
All rights reserved
Published simultaneously in Canada by HarperCollins *CanadaLtd*
Printed in the United States of America
Designed by Amy Samson
First edition, 1995

Library of Congress Cataloging-in-Publication Data
Ferris, Jean.
Signs of life / Jean Ferris. — 1st ed.
p.   cm.
[1. Death—Fiction. 2. Family problems—Fiction.
3. Man, Prehistoric—Fiction. 4. Lascaux Cave (France)—Fiction.]
I. Title.
PZ7.F4175Si 1994 [Fic]—dc20 94-28709 CIP AC

For Larry Dane Brimner, Sheila Cole,
and Kathy Krull, co-conspirators

Signs of Life

One

"Five . . . four . . . three . . . two . . . one . . . Happy New Year!" I yelled, and threw my arms around Mark. Illicit champagne bubbles were in my head and in my veins, and I felt as if, in this new year, the year in which I would become seventeen, I could fly, I could turn sand to gold, I could do anything I could think up. I kissed Mark with all the strength and fire of my new possibilities. He cooperated admirably.

An arm slid around my waist, and I turned. I knew who it would be: Molly. Molly, my twin in everything external and almost nothing internal. Although six minutes younger than I, she seemed far older—calm, thoughtful, careful, with a sly sense of humor and a genius for solving problems of any kind, algebraic or interpersonal. I was excitable, impulsive, restless, with a loud laugh and a penchant for creating the kind of problems that Molly was so good at solving. We were both blue-eyed, with shoulder-length brown hair, but where hers was smooth and shining and softly turned under, mine was streaked with self-administered blond highlights, permed into a pile of curls, and worn pulled up off my neck.

"Happy New Year, Duplicate," Molly said, and hugged me.

I hugged her back. "To you, too, Clone."

Mark gave her a peck on the cheek, which she endured. She didn't like Mark, didn't think he was good for me because he was such an enthusiastic partier. She'd have liked him even less if she'd known about the bottle of champagne that he and I had been drinking in his car, and planned to polish off later.

Peter Rand, Molly's steady boyfriend, junior class president and Westinghouse Science Fair winner with some incomprehensible project about genetic codes, gave me a chaste and hasty kiss. He felt the same way about me that Molly felt about Mark, and for the same reasons.

But no matter our opinions of each other's boyfriends, hairdos, or food preferences, we were still twins, joined since the moment of our conception, and I knew we'd stay up, whatever time we got home tonight, reliving this party that we were experiencing in such different ways. I couldn't wait to hear what Molly had to say about Sara Kim's awful pink outfit, or listen to her imitate Brittany Prentice's neighing laugh.

"Is this the year you get an eagle tattooed on your bicep?" Molly asked me, grinning. "Or is this the year you become a spirit channeler?"

"Why can't I do both?" I asked. "I don't like to close any doors." Nothing was truer than that. Between acting in all the Drama Club productions, being on the pep squad, working on the yearbook, and dating Mark, I hardly knew what an idle moment was.

Molly shook her head, while Mark laughed.

"What will you do this year?" I asked her. "Qualify for sainthood?"

"Oh, I hope so," she said. "My halo size is six and a half if you want to get me a canonization present."

My mother thought it was terrible the way we treated each other as opposite poles of behavior, Molly the saint and me the sinner, even though that's how she herself seemed to regard us. My father said it was our way of establishing our individual identities, and it was important psychological work. Molly and I thought it was funny.

"Peter and I are leaving pretty soon," Molly said. "When do you think you'll be home?"

"By three, on pain of death," I said. We'd fought hard with my mother to get her to give us such a late curfew for New Year's Eve. I knew Molly had been fighting mostly for me; staying out until three would never be her idea of a good time. She and Peter would probably go someplace for an espresso or a Coke and be home by one, when he would kiss her properly, once, under the porch light. She'd go in to brush and floss her teeth, write in her diary, and wait for me to show up with champagne on my breath and my Party Pink lipstick kissed entirely off.

"Okay," she said. "See you then, Duplicate."

"Later, Clone."

Mark and I danced for a while longer, not just with each other, but with everyone, and then went out to his car to cool off and then heat up again, and then drink our champagne. It was warm and flat and I couldn't finish even one glass, but I felt as giddy and light-headed as if I'd drunk the whole bottle.

"Oh, my gosh," I said, looking at my watch. "It's almost three. I've got to get home." Despite my nonchalance about other things, I was never late for a curfew. For some reason, that was the one area where I tried to avoid my mother's wrath, always harsher on me than on Molly. Of course, Molly rarely aroused much anger, and I often did.

Mark drove, too fast as usual, while I straightened my clothes and brushed my hair. It was unlikely that Mother or Dad would be waiting up for me, but you never knew. Once in a while they did, and it was best to be prepared.

Mark pulled up in front of my house behind another car at exactly two minutes before three. "Well done," I said.

"So now we have two minutes to squander," he said. "Come here." He put his hand on my shoulder.

I shook my head. "Enough," I said. "Save something for tomorrow." I looked out the car window and noticed that every light in the downstairs of my house was on. And the front door was opening.

My father came down the porch steps two at a time and ran to Mark's car. He pulled open the passenger door and leaned in. "Hannah," he said. "Thank God."

"What?" I asked, alarmed.

"Is that a police car?" Mark asked, pointing to the car he'd parked behind.

The lamplight from the porch reflected on the tears in my father's eyes and I knew. "Molly," I said, with the complete knowledge that now I had a problem she'd never be able to solve. That nobody could solve.

The tears in my father's eyes brimmed and spilled, while every tear in me turned to ice.

Two

I jerked awake before I could scream, the way I had that night six months ago and the way I sometimes still did when I dreamed of it, over and over, in an attempt to change the ending in my mind and in reality.

I was crammed, sweating, in the corner of the backseat of the rented Citroën, my head bumping against the window glass, as my father drove the winding country road and my mother peered at the map. The other side of the seat, where Molly should have been, was piled with the sweaters and raincoats we shed as we made our way from cool, rainy Paris to the perfect June summer of the Dordogne in southern France.

We'd come because of a movie my father had seen as a boy, a movie he said had shown him what he wanted to be when he grew up. In the movie—which Molly and I had rented once and thought was silly, with laughably clumsy special effects—an anthropologist found dinosaur eggs in a cave in the Dordogne. He hatched them into unruly pets, which made a lot of trouble, until they were shipped off to some remote island with a big, about-to-erupt volcano. My father, who was now an anthropologist, had always wanted to come here and look at the caves. In what became a private joke among us, he promised Molly and me our own dinosaurs if he was ever lucky enough to find those prehistoric eggs. For years we'd all listened to him talk about the wondrous painted cave of Lascaux, his favorite of all the Dordogne's ancient caves, some painted, some not, and speculate about how the people who made that art had lived, and how much like us they might have been. But we'd never before managed to organize an actual trip.

Instead, we spent every summer since Molly and I were born at our Lake Arrowhead cottage, from which Mother and Dad had taken turns commuting to the city to teach their summer-school classes at UCLA. Until this summer, when none of us had wanted to go where we might find a faded bathing suit of Molly's in the warped bureau drawer, a curling photo of her stuck in the mirror inside the front door, the tennis shoes she'd left behind in our final packing frenzy last summer. This summer we'd finally come to France, looking not just for caves but for the impossible: the illusion that our lives were the same as they'd always been.

"Read me those directions again, Mother," my father said to my mother. "I think we must be getting close."

My mother read. Her voice was her best feature, warm and vibrant and full of excitement. It was one of the things that made her chemistry lectures so popular. Almost every semester, some infatuated male sophomore wrote her a note of admiration mentioning her voice. She always brought the notes proudly home. To me, that voice seemed to have been accidentally transplanted from someone who really *was* warm and vibrant and full of enthusiasm into my mother, who only got excited about chemistry. And about Molly.

We approached a village made of the golden stone the region was famous for, the buildings covered with flowering vines, all impossibly quaint. I knew I didn't want to be at the lake this summer, but neither did I want to be traveling with my parents, having culture and picturesqueness forced on me. I understood that they were trying to distract me, and themselves, to speed the healing process, to pretend we weren't missing Molly. But it wouldn't work. I was never going to heal, so there was no point in these elaborate efforts. I wanted to be home, where at least I could have my nightmares in familiar surroundings. My nights, with their vivid dreams of Molly alive, even with their vivid dreams of Molly's death, now had a greater allure for me than my days, with activities that seemed meaningless in the face of my impossible loss. I'd gradually quit doing anything but drifting from class to class in a haze so thick that I barely noticed the withdrawal of my friends, who didn't know how to be with me anymore.

"Here, on the right," my mother said, her voice making the words sound like the start of a song. The tribute she read at Molly's funeral would have brought the audience to tears even if she'd done it in Chinese; understanding her words just made the tears flow faster. I was the only one there who hadn't cried. And still hadn't.

My father turned through an archway of tawny stone into a paved parking area. The pretty, old hotel surrounded us on three sides, windows open to the bright air, window boxes a riot of geraniums and spicy summer scents. The front door was open, and two cats were laid out in the sun on the top step like doormats. We had to step over their warm, inert bodies to get inside.

We had adjoining rooms at the back of the hotel, with tiny balconies overlooking the Vézère River, which whispered past below us. My room was decorated with pink cabbage roses on the bedspread, wallpaper, and upholstered chair. There were real pink roses in a pewter mug on the dresser. They were overblown, the way I like them best, past the point of restrained perfection that Molly preferred.

My father knocked on the door that connected our two rooms. When I answered, he opened the door. "Want to go with me to get tomorrow's tickets for Lascaux? We could have lunch somewhere along the way."

"Is Mother going?"

"No." He paused. "She thought she'd take a nap and have lunch here when she feels like it."

Practically all my mother had done since January was sleep, rousing herself only to go teach her classes. She'd even gone straight to bed after Molly's funeral, in spite of our houseful of people. Maybe her dreams were of Molly, too.

"I think I'll do the same," I said, though I had no intention of sleeping. I'd already dreamed once today about New Year's Eve, about the randomness of a drunk driver plowing into Peter's car a block from our house.

The champagne I drank with Mark was the last alcohol I'd had since that night. Not that it changed anything, except that Mark was going with somebody else, someone more fun than I was now. Really, I didn't blame him. I'd lost interest in him, too, along with everything else.

After my father had gone and all was quiet in my parents' room, I went down the stairs and left the hotel, stepping over the cats again. I walked through the town, which was drowsing in the hot sunlight. Because I couldn't read the signs over the shops, or understand the people I passed, I felt nearly invisible, drifting like smoke through an alien place. It was past lunchtime, but I wasn't hungry and didn't stop anywhere to eat.

Vineyards came close to the edges of the village, and to meadows of grazing sheep and cattle. The golden gravel-paved side streets turned gradually into dirt lanes leading to farmhouses. Along one of these lanes I leaned on a fence, watching cows grazing. I imagined having a job that required me to do nothing but eat all day, mindless and serene. Sounded pretty good, except that I didn't want to end up the way cows did.

I moved to another fence beside another pasture where sheep grazed. One looked up at me, and within seconds they were all staring at me, their jaws grinding sideways as they gawked. Then the first one returned to her meal, and so did they all. When another sheep made a turn and wandered a bit to the left, they all followed her like . . . well, like sheep. They looked so sweet and dopey that I laughed aloud. They all raised their heads and looked at me, more baffled than curious, and I laughed again.

Over their heads, I caught sight, several meadows away, of bright pennants fluttering lazily from the peaks of what looked like a circus tent. I remembered the posters I'd seen in the town, big black letters at the top announcing LE CIRQUE D'ÉTÉ. Maybe Dad and I could go to the circus one night. I doubted that my mother would want to come with us.

Sunlight poured over me, heavy and hot as lava, and I

decided to walk back to the hotel in the shade of the poplar trees by the river.

The sound of the water was soothing; the sight of it, silvery and shimmering, seemed to lower my temperature even more. The person I'd been before Molly died might have stepped into the cool current, shorts, T-shirt, and all, without a thought. The frozen empty person I'd become considered it and declined.

Three

As I stood watching the water glide by, I heard a rapid slapping sound I couldn't identify. I walked along the path, cautious, and the sound grew louder. Then, in a space between the trees, dappled with shade, I saw a broad-shouldered man, his back to me. He had curly black hair and wore jeans and a red shirt. Over his head a circuit of sparkling colored rings whirled, each hitting his palm with a smack for an instant before he sent it up again. As I watched, he dropped one of the rings. His rhythm broken, he tried to catch all the remaining ones, but two others fell, one of them rolling across the grass to my feet. When he turned, muttering, to retrieve it, he saw me and straightened, saying something in French.

Face-on, I could see he wasn't a man, not quite yet. He was my age, or a little older, olive-skinned, with heavy black eyelashes framing obsidian-dark eyes. He spoke again in French.

I shrugged and smiled. "I don't speak French," I said. "I'm American."

"American!" he exclaimed in English. "Where are you from in America?" His English was flawless, not even a trace of an accent, though there was something in the cadence of his words that made them sound slightly foreign.

"California. Los Angeles."

"Someday I'm going to see California," he said, and the trace of a frown flickered over his face and was gone.

"You must be with the circus," I said, handing him the yellow ring that had rolled to my feet.

"Oh, you know of us? Le Cirque d'Été? It's my family's circus, the Kremo Family's Circus of Summer. We should be gone by now, on to Toulouse, but our truck is broken—the big one that carries the tent. We're waiting for a part to come, and while we wait, we perform every night. Everyone for miles around has seen us. Soon we'll be inviting in the cows and the sheep."

"You'd only have to invite one sheep," I said.

He gave me a grin that made me think of buccaneers and Gypsy campfires. "Yes," he said. "The rest will follow her. They are such . . ."

"Sheep," I finished.

We stood smiling at each other for a moment. Then he raised his arms and the air over his head was full of the spinning rings, sending out flashes of color from the sunlight off their spangles.

At circuses I'd always been too far away from the performers to feel a part of what they were doing. Here the magic was just for me, an audience of one. And I always thought that what the performers did looked easy, their skill denying the difficulty. Here I could see the beads of sweat on the boy's forehead and upper lip, the set of his jaw in concentration, the way his eyes followed the rings up and then down. What he did looked hard, and that he could do it so fluidly seemed nearly miraculous.

I clapped my hands and he dropped a ring. He cursed—at least I assumed it was a curse; it was in a language I didn't recognize.

"I'm sorry," I said. "I didn't mean to distract you."

"It wasn't you," he said. "I perform before noisy crowds all the time. It was this." He held his right hand out to me. There was an open sore at the base of his thumb where the rings hit every time he caught one. I winced at the sight of it and wondered how he managed to catch the rings even once.

"Why don't you bandage it?" I asked.

"I can't catch as well. And I must continue to practice, to improve. Anyone can throw five rings. A lot can do seven. Hardly anybody can do nine. I want to do nine."

"I couldn't do five," I said.

"I could teach you," he said.

"I don't think so. My mother says I'm the clumsiest person alive. I have—had—a sister who got all the graceful genes."

"No," he said flatly. "No," he said again, bending to pick up a string bag that lay under a tree along with a couple of books. "Your mother is wrong." He took three plums from the bag and put one of them into my right hand. "Throw it up and catch it," he said.

"Like this?" I asked, doing as he'd said.

"Exactly like that. Keep on." He watched me toss the plum a few times. It made a wet-sounding *splat* in my palm every time it landed, and I hoped it had a thick skin.

• 15 •

Then he put a plum into my left hand. "Same thing," he said.

"At the same time?" I asked, wondering if this was going to be like trying to pat my head and rub my stomach simultaneously.

"If you can."

I tried it. Both plums went up at the same time and came down, splat, at the same time into my palms.

"Very good. Again."

I did it a few more times.

"Now throw them to the opposite hands, one starting a little before the other."

Nothing to it, though the plums were beginning to feel rather liquid inside their skins. "Is this how you learned to juggle?" I asked him, concentrating on my flying plums.

"Exactly how. But I was six when I started, not . . . how old are you?"

I almost said sixteen. It was hard for me to understand that Molly and I would never be the same age again. "Seventeen."

"Ah," he said. "A very old lady to begin juggling. But perhaps you are a natural. I think maybe so."

I laughed and dropped a plum. It broke open on the ground in a gold and purple mess.

"I think maybe not," I said.

He took the remaining plum from my hand and threw it in a high arc, through the trees, into the river. His red sleeve slid over the contracting and relaxing muscles in his arm, and I realized how tired my arms were. I couldn't imagine the hours of practice that had gone into the building of those muscles, into the expertise with which he handled the rings.

He tossed me the third plum. "You might as well eat it," he said. "Not much juggling you can do with one plum."

I bit into it, hungry at last, and the juice ran down my chin. I thought I had never tasted a plum so sweet and warm from the sun. "Where did you learn to speak such perfect English?" I asked him.

"From traveling with the circus. It sounds perfect to you? Good. I want to speak English best, though I speak five other languages, too: French, Spanish, Italian, German, and Romany, of course."

"Romany? What's that?"

"You didn't know I'm what you call a Gypsy? Romany is our language."

"You're a Gypsy?" He'd already seemed impossibly exotic, and now he confirmed it.

"It's a word we don't use about ourselves," he said. "We are Roma. Or sometimes we call ourselves Travelers. Others call us Gypsies. It's not often a complimentary word."

In Paris we'd been warned to watch out for crowds of Gypsies who would surround us and steal from us, but we hadn't seen any, and I'd thought the hotel manager was just being dramatic. To me, Gypsies—not that I actually knew anything about them—were romantic figures, not criminals, with doomed love affairs and spirited dances around campfires, kings and fortune-tellers with painted caravans.

"So Le Cirque d'Été is all Gypsies? Are they really all your family?"

He nodded. "Aunts, uncles, cousins. And others we call family, but can't really say how we are related. I was born into the circus. My father is the strong man. He does trapeze, acrobatics, balancing. When I was three I was doing one-handed handstands on his head. My mother flies—the trapeze—and trains the dogs and the horses. We all do more than one thing. And we live on the road."

The thought of endless traveling with my parents was enough to make me faint with dread.

"My name is Stefan Kremo," he said, giving me a little bow and holding out his hand.

"Hannah Flood." I shook his hand, gently because it was the one with the wound.

"Will you sit?" He gestured toward the tree his string bag and books lay under. "I've eaten my lunch already, I'm afraid, but there's some mineral water and some bread left. May I offer you?"

I sat, oddly touched by his formal hospitality in spite of his meager offerings. "Thank you," I said, accepting a piece of bread and a freshly opened liter of water.

"And you are here to see the caves," he said, seating himself and clasping his hands around his knees.

"How did you know?" I asked with my mouth full of wonderful crusty French bread.

"Everyone comes here to see the caves. And to eat foie gras and truffles, which are both as costly as jewels. While I love foie gras, in spite of how it is made, truffles taste only musty to me. Lucky for me, since I couldn't afford them anyway."

Suddenly I wished I'd done some homework for this trip and knew more about the area other than the caves, which I'd been hearing about all my life. Instead, I'd been dragged along like a piece of especially heavy luggage. I had no idea what foie gras and truffles were.

"Uh, how is foie gras made?" I asked.

He gave me a sidelong look. "I hesitate to tell you, but you will probably see it if you stay here very long. It is called *le gavage*. The geese are force-fed warm maize through a funnel down their throats, until their livers are enlarged by as much as six times. Diseased, I suppose you could say. Then they are slaughtered and the pâté is made from these livers." He shrugged. "I like it, even knowing that."

Pâté de foie gras, I knew then, was one delicacy I would be avoiding for the rest of my life. I decided not to even ask about truffles.

"We're going to Lascaux tomorrow," I said, changing the subject. "Have you been there?"

"Oh, yes," he said. "You don't see the real cave, you know, only a replica. But the replica is perfect."

"We came all this way and we don't get to see the real cave? Why not?"

"Because people weren't good for it when it was open to the public. Their breath, and what they brought in on their shoes, changed the atmosphere. Made it damper, full of carbon dioxide, infected with bacteria. This poison harmed the beautiful paintings. So now the real cave is closed except to a few scientists. But the replica is perfect, even the same bumps on the wall, the same materials used to paint the pictures. You'll be amazed." He offered me another piece of bread, which I accepted.

"What do you do in the circus?" I asked him.

He grinned. "Everything. Put up the tent, take it down. Wash Babette—that's the elephant. Clean up after the horses."

"What about the juggling?"

"Well, that, too. And some tightrope. And I'm a clown."

"I don't know why you need all those relatives. It sounds as if you and your parents could do the whole thing by yourselves."

He smiled and lay back in the grass. "Life in the circus is almost like the religious life. Every day we move, yet every day's the same; there's a routine you can count on, and other people living the same life alongside you. And we make magic. For ninety minutes we can make people forget their lives—we take them to another place. Sometimes what I do is drudgery, and sometimes I feel it is almost sacred."

I lay back, too, and looked up into the leaves of the poplar trees. They moved sluggishly in the hot breeze. In Los Angeles, lying in the grass in an isolated place with a total stranger—a *male* total stranger—would have been insanity. Maybe it was here, too, but for some reason I didn't think so. How likely was it that serial killers would disarm their victims with juggling lessons and talk of pâté de foie gras?

"But don't you miss a regular life—a house, school, friends?" I asked, I who was missing my own regular life, the life that would not be coming back to me.

"Yes." He sighed. "But the only way to have that is to leave the circus, leave my family. Become *merimay*. I don't know if I could ever do that."

"*Merimay?*" I asked.

"Defiled. Unclean. Cast out. It would be as if I were more than dead to them if I went to live as a *gadje*, a non-Gypsy." He paused. "They would never again say my name."

"What do you mean, more than dead?" I asked. "And why would they never say your name?" *Never* was a concept I'd been trying, since New Year's Eve, to get used to. So was *dead.*

He sat up and clasped his hands around his knees again. His face was grave. "If I died they'd be able to say my name for a year. That's how long it takes the ghost, the *mulo*, to join the ancestors in the Place of Unborn Souls. After a year, with the proper mourning and remembrance feasts, the *mulo* is supposed to be resigned to being dead. But there's always the danger of calling it back after that by saying its name, so we don't. We're just glad it's with the ancestors and we honor them all, without using names, at a yearly ceremony. But if a member of my family goes away from the Roma, leaves voluntarily, it's as if he never existed."

"That would be hard," I said, wondering how seriously he was thinking about leaving. I picked up the two books from under the tree and looked at the spines. They were in English. "Accounting?" I asked. "Computer programming? Do you want to keep the accounts for the circus, too, on top of everything else you do?"

He took one of the books from me and flipped the pages. "Like English, like music, numbers are an international language. Accounting, computers—if I can speak those languages, I can go anywhere, work anywhere."

Evidently he was seriously considering becoming more than dead.

"Isn't juggling an international language, too?"

He looked up at me, brighter. "It is. You should see some of the really good jugglers. They can get all the balls in the air and do tumbling while they wait for the balls to come down. They balance things on their heads and their chins while they juggle. They juggle on the tightwire. With knives. With fire. In the circus, flaming is always better than not," he added. "My cousin juggles an entire formal dinner, with the food, the candles, even the table. He's fantastic." He looked at his watch and stood up. "I have to go," he said. "Come see the circus tonight." He took a ticket from his back pocket and put it into my hand. "You're my guest. Professional courtesy to a fellow performer."

"Thanks. I'll try to come. Maybe I'll bring a sheep."

He laughed, then put his books into the string bag, slung the handles over his shoulder, and cut through the trees to the main road. As he crossed it, the sparkling rings appeared, spinning over his head, flashing and blurring. I watched him go, his wide shoulders swinging easily, the afternoon sun warming his black curls.

Four

My father was in the lobby when I got back to the hotel. "I was about to come looking for you," he said. "Where have you been?"

Since Molly's death, Dad worried more about me than he used to. It was understandable, of course, but useless. All the worry in the world couldn't have helped Molly.

"I took a walk. There's a circus over in the meadow, a Gypsy family circus."

My father frowned. "Remember what we were told in Paris about Gypsies."

"I don't believe it. At least, not about all Gypsies. Just because people are poor doesn't mean they have to be criminals."

My father looked at me thoughtfully. "You're right, of course. Well, I'm glad you had a nice afternoon. Did you have lunch here at the hotel?"

"No." I didn't know why, but I wanted to keep Stefan a secret. Everything about him: his seraph's face, his strong, wounded hand, his gentle way of teaching me, all seemed too strange and mysterious to try to explain. "Did you get the tickets for Lascaux?"

He pulled them from his shirt pocket. "I got them for a morning tour, in case your mother wants to rest after lunch. A lot of the tickets go to tour groups, so I was smart to get them now."

"You're always smart, Daddy," I said, taking his arm in mine and rubbing my cheek against his shoulder. My mother teased him about being an absentminded professor, but I'd take his sweet preoccupation over her head-on control any day.

Even his grief over Molly was in character, straightforward and bone-deep. Sometimes he stood in the doorway to her room and let tears run down his cheeks and off his chin as if he didn't even know they were there. Once I found him sitting in his car in the garage, bent over the steering wheel, sobbing. But after these episodes of sorrow, he would straighten himself up and go about preparing a lecture or paying bills or mowing the lawn until the next time, weaving his grief into his life in a way I wished I could.

I, true to *my* nature, ran from it by trying to become someone else, a person without a life, without emotions. My mother slept. Dad was the only one of the three of us who seemed to be making any kind of progress.

"Yes, indeed, I am, and don't you forget it," he said. "Now let's go see what your mother's been up to."

"Do you think you'd like to go to the circus tonight?" I asked. "I don't believe you have to understand French to understand a circus."

He gave me a squeeze. "Well, of course *you* must go. It'll be part of your whole French experience. I'll come, too, if Mother's interested." He'd only begun to call her

Mother instead of Anne after Molly died, as if he needed to remind himself of her role as a mother, even though her child was gone. I wondered if he felt, as I did, that she had always been more Molly's mother than mine.

My mother had slept all afternoon and sat up groggily when we came into the room. "It's the heat," she said. "It puts me right out."

After dinner she said she was still feeling lethargic and declined the circus. "Maybe tomorrow night," she said. "But you go, Alex," she said to my father. "Don't let me keep you away."

"I think I'll stay in tonight," he said. "I want to read up on Lascaux. But I'll walk Hannah over, just to make sure she gets there all right."

With such ease he gave us each his loyalty. When affection is real, as my father's was, it expresses itself instinctively. With my mother, I often had the sense that before she responded to me she asked herself, "What would her real mother say in this situation?"

My father and I walked through the warm, starlit night. We could hear the river behind us, its silver sound growing fainter and fainter as we made our way through meadows smelling of something unfamiliar and pungent. Cars passed us, squeezing along the narrow lane, led by the strings of lights along the tent edges and the sound of calliope music.

My father sighed. "Circus music's the same all over the world," he said. "Strauss and Wagner and Sousa. The only things that kind of music should make you think of are circuses and parades. The *Radetzky March* makes me feel twelve again."

"Are you sure you won't stay?" I asked. He sounded

so wistful, I wanted to give him his very own circus gift-wrapped.

"No, no. Mother's expecting me back. You enjoy yourself. Maybe we'll come tomorrow." He patted my shoulder. "There'll be plenty of people leaving when you do. You should be perfectly safe walking back to the hotel. But I could come for you if you . . ." He trailed off.

"I'll be fine," I said, making the kind of promise he didn't believe anymore.

"Okay. Well, knock on my door when you get back, just so I know."

I said I would. Then I watched his tall, slightly stoop-shouldered figure retreat, fading away from the lights and the music.

The area in front of the tent was full of people purchasing tickets while their children ran and shrieked in a delirium of excitement, then peered, awestruck, around the side of the tent, where Babette stood in her gold and scarlet trappings waiting to go on, amazingly big, especially if you were little. Stefan wouldn't have to invite the sheep in yet; there still seemed to be plenty of local enthusiasm for Le Cirque d'Été.

I gave my ticket to a boy of about ten who stood importantly at the entrance, collecting tickets and pointing to seats. He looked enough like Stefan to have *been* him at that age.

My seat was in the front row, so close that I felt a part of the show. I could see that the paint was chipped on the ring curb; I could smell the hay and sawdust filling the single ring; I could see the size of the stakes driven into the ground to hold up the trapeze rig, and hoped that they were big enough.

I could have been anywhere, in any country, surrounded by the familiar sounds of excited children, the smells of animals and sweat, and the nearly breathless sense of anticipation, waiting for the magic to begin, waiting for the ninety minutes that would, as Stefan promised, take me to another place, far away from my life.

A fanfare of music made us all sit up straighter, and the children hushed. The spotlight settled on a man in a red coat, white jodhpurs, boots, and a top hat, a whip in his hand. I couldn't understand what he said, but I'm sure it was something like, "Ladies and gentlemen, boys and girls, children of all ages, welcome to Le Cirque d'Été."

The parade began, Babette in the lead, ridden by a beautiful girl about my age, dressed in red and gold, her hat a tower of plumes. The clowns came next, throwing candy to the audience and tripping in an exaggerated way over their big shoes. There were horses and a donkey and a pack of lively dogs. The aerialists marched along in tights and sequins; the acrobats tumbled and back-flipped; a man in blue kept a flock of doves flying over his head; and a group of kids rode on unicycles. I looked for Stefan but didn't see him. If he was one of the clowns, I didn't recognize him in his makeup.

The parade went around the ring several times before it began to file out again, and on the last pass one of the clowns, in overalls and a purple wig, with a piglet on a leash, stopped before my seat and produced a bunch of red paper roses from somewhere. He handed me the bouquet and whipped out another one, which he also handed me. The spotlight found us, and the band began to play a romantic waltz with a clownish syncopated rhythm. Faster than I could take hold of them, the clown produced more bouquets, pink and blue and yellow and lavender, heaping them in my lap and at my feet. It had to be Stefan. I laughed and gathered up the fake flowers.

Stefan patted his big gloved hand over his heart and fluttered his eyelashes, pretending dizziness as he handed me flowers. The whole audience was watching, whistling and shouting encouragement as the last of the parade left the tent. The spotlight followed them to the exit, then came back to Stefan and me and the flowers, jerking impatiently away as the little orchestra made fretful sounds, urging Stefan to move on.

Children yelled to the clown, probably telling him he was supposed to go, though of course I couldn't understand them. He appeared oblivious, leaning over to me, offering me his piglet once his supply of flowers was gone. I was about to take it when several clowns came running back in, pulling a big red wagon. They grabbed Stefan and the piglet, and after a lot of wrestling, falling, and funny noises, they got Stefan into the wagon. One sat on him as they hustled him out of the tent to tremendous applause, leaving me buried in paper flowers. Unexpected tears welled in my eyes. I didn't care how many times Stefan might have done this trick before, in other towns, with other girls. Tonight, to me, it was fresh and sweet, and reminded me that once I'd taken happiness and pleasure for granted, thinking they could never end.

Le Cirque d'Été was a good circus, full of energetic and talented people and well-trained animals, too. But horses running in unison, jumping through hoops, even flaming hoops, and standing on their hind legs, just didn't get me excited. I laughed at the dogs riding on the goat's back and playing basketball, but at the same time I felt sorry for them, doing something for reasons they couldn't understand, just trying to please their masters.

But it was Stefan I watched most closely. He returned, still in his clown costume, carrying his piglet, blowing bubbles into the crowd. The ringmaster came up to him and spoke sternly, screwing the cap back on the bottle of bubble water. Stefan slunk to the other side of the ring, where he blew more bubbles. Several times the ringmaster caught him and scolded him. Finally the ringmaster took the bottle of bubbles from Stefan, throwing it into a trash can. He walked away, dusting his hands with satisfaction.

Stefan looked sadly at the closed trash can, walked dejectedly around it several times, then looked furtively over his shoulder for the ringmaster. When he didn't see him, he pulled the lid off the trash can. A fountain of bubbles erupted, blown into the audience on all sides by hidden fans. The bubbles kept coming and Stefan stood among them, wonder-struck, holding his piglet and pointing to the bubbles. He touched a bubble, and when it popped, it made a musical note. Astonishment and joy appeared on his face. Then, popping one bubble after another with his finger, he played a little tune with them. The children in the audience tried it, too, as the bubbles drifted over them. They didn't have an orchestra helping them, but they were enchanted nonetheless. And so was I.

After several more acts, Stefan appeared again, this time on the tightrope, still in his clown costume, carrying his rings. He stopped in the middle of the rope, where he juggled the rings. Then he let them drop to the ground and he turned backflips and somersaults, and I held my breath. While he did the tricks, he removed pieces of his outfit, sometimes in midair, until he was left in only his wig, baggy striped long johns, and socks. He gingerly removed one sock, teetering and overbalancing. When he bent to remove the other sock, he fell, tumbling over himself into the net as the children screamed. He bounced back up onto the wire, sock in hand, beaming bemusedly while we all yelled "Bravo!"

At the end, each performer came back for a final bow and tour around the tent as the band played and the audience clapped in rhythm with it. Stefan ran about in his long underwear, throwing kisses to the audience. When he got to me, he pulled another bunch of flowers from the buttoned-up seat of his drawers and, as he handed it to me, said, "Wait right here," and scampered off.

Could any girl refuse an invitation like that?

While the people filed out, I sat among my flowers, watching some of Stefan's relatives already raking out the ring and taking down the aerialists' net. In a few minutes Stefan returned, in jeans and a T-shirt, his face washed. "Did you like it?" he asked.

"It was wonderful. Especially the flowers."

"You're supposed to say, 'Especially *you*,'" he said. "Anybody can give you flowers."

"Especially you," I said agreeably. "I loved the piglet. I loved the act with the bubbles."

"I like that one, too," he said.

I started to hand him back his flowers, but he said, "Keep them. To remember Le Cirque d'Été. They fold up—that's how I get them in my costume." He showed me how to collapse them and pulled a plastic bag from his pocket for me to put them all into.

I stood up. "Thank you for the ticket. It was a great evening."

"Come back tomorrow."

"Maybe I will. If you're still here."

"We will be. The truck isn't fixed yet." He hesitated and then went on. "Will you come on a picnic with me tomorrow? I'll bring Fifi, my piglet. We can take a canoe on the river."

"I'd like that," I said. "We're going to Lascaux in the morning, but we'll be back by lunch. Should I come here, or meet you at the river?"

He thought for a moment. "Come here. I'll see you tomorrow. Sleep well." He gave me a salute and took up a rake to help in the ring.

I walked back to the hotel, following the last of the cars leaving the circus grounds. I took out a bunch of the trick flowers, opened them, and held them under my nose as if they actually had a smell. Maybe tonight, for the first night in months, I would sleep well, without the dreams of Molly that were both consolation and torment. Or would I be wakeful with guilt for the fun I'd had with Stefan, the kind of fun that Molly would never get to have?

Five

The cave was empty, dark, and dank. And freezing cold, with a strong smell of lion. But there were piles of bones that were old and dry and would burn well. There were fresher bones as well, some with meat still on them.

She knew she had to hurry. There was no way to tell when the lion would come back. But it was her job to bring fuel for the fires, and at last she had found a rich source. Because the winter had been unusually cold and wet, there was no dry wood left anywhere near the camp.

She carried armloads of bones outside the cave mouth and piled them a short distance away, in a place where she could get to them even after the lion returned, and take them in relays back to the camp.

The winter had been so long she thought it was never going to end. Maybe this time it wouldn't. Maybe Earth-the-Mother had decided that now She liked winter and wanted it to stay.

The prospect of living the rest of her life bundled into her skins and furs, spending the whole day scavenging for fuel and something to eat, and the night shivering around the small fires, was more than she could endure. She loved the summer, when they moved into the river valley—where they could swim every day, where fish and game and firewood were abundant, where they prepared for the initiation ceremonies.

Summer had to come again.

She heard a sound at the mouth of the cave and knew instantly and too late that she had been foolish again, dreaming of summer instead of remembering the ways of winter. One had to negotiate winter one careful step at a time, paying attention all the way.

She stood still and listened. It was the cave lion, there was no mistake. She'd have known it just by its smell, even if its bulk hadn't blocked what little gray light filtered around the bend in the cave to where she stood. And if she could smell the lion, it could smell her.

So this was how she would die and go to the Old Ones. There would be no more summers for her. No goodbyes, no one to breathe in her last breath, no more anything. She'd never finish learning how to make the colors, how to paint the animal spirits on the cave walls. And worse, she would be one of those who were lost, whose bones were never found by anyone, who disappeared as if they'd never been.

The lion was still, listening, at the bend in the cave. His smell was strong in her nostrils and she could hear his breathing. Then he moved, slowly lifting his big paws, coming forward, looking for her.

She knew exactly when he saw her. His great head was at a level with hers and he raised it until the gleam of his eyes met hers. She squeezed her eyes closed and then opened them. It was useless. Even if he couldn't see the shine of her eyes, he could see the shape of her shadow, smell her, sense her. If she was to die this way, she wanted to see it coming. Waiting in the darkness of her own closed eyes like a coward was intolerable. Even if no one else would ever know how she died, she would.

She stood straighter, squaring her shoulders, holding a stack of bones before her. The bones rattled in her shaking arms and she braced her elbows into her sides to stop the shivering.

The lion might be hungry, too. There was a strange comfort in knowing that her death would feed his life, that her spirit would continue, in a way, in him.

The lion sprang, roaring, straight at her. Her heart seemed to stop in her chest, and her limbs went hot and loose. Her head rang with the sound of his roar reverberating off the cave walls. In a reflex of defiance, she threw the pile of bones at the lion just as he hit her, his claws raking through the thicknesses of her skins and furs and into her flesh. Blood is so warm, *she thought as the lion's fangs struck her shoulder.*

Six

I woke in the dark with a jerk. I was sitting upright in my bed, my hands extended in front of me, sweat causing the T-shirt I slept in to stick to my skin. A sound echoed in the room, and I didn't know if it came from the dream or from my own throat.

Gradually my breathing slowed and I remembered the dream: a huge lion in a cave, springing, sinking its claws and fangs into me. How could I have had such a dream when I'd gone to sleep happier than I'd been in six months? I expected dreams—they always came—but dreams of Molly, not cave lions. Was I so suggestible that the nearness of prehistoric caves made me dream of them? Or was this somehow a disguised Molly-dream? A dream in which I paid for the pleasures I could still have, which were denied to Molly.

I got up, my T-shirt damp against me, and went to the open window. I had no idea what time it was, but the darkness outside was complete, barely relieved by starshine. The river below murmured softly, as if whispering secrets.

In my room, Stefan's paper flowers, opened again, were all over, stuck behind the mirror, strewn across the tabletop, on the windowsill, competing with the cabbage roses in the decor. It made me smile even now to know they were there in the dark.

I changed into a dry T-shirt, straightened my bed, and lay down again, looking at the ceiling until the darkness beyond the windows turned gray and then lemony and then clear. When my father knocked on our adjoining door to wake me, I was already dressed, sitting in the chair by the window, my lap full of paper roses.

Just after breakfast, the three of us got into the car for the ride to Lascaux.

"How was the circus last night?" my father asked. "I thought sometimes I could hear the music drifting on the breeze."

"It was great. You have to come tonight. It's only one ring, so you can watch everything, and the performers are really good." I paused. "One of the clowns is especially talented."

"Clowning is a real art," he said. "It's hard to be funny without being offensive, to be funny enough for grownups without losing the kids, and to have that little touch of poignancy I always like. Red Skelton had that." He sighed.

"Nobody knows who Red Skelton is anymore," my mother said. "Think of somebody else. Jay Leno. Jerry Seinfeld."

"Who?" Dad asked.

"I've heard of Red Skelton," I said, feeling as if I had to defend Dad for not watching enough TV.

"Do you think you'd like to go tonight, Mother?" my father asked.

"I don't know. But you go, anyway, even if I don't want to."

"I'd rather you came," he said. He persisted in trying to draw her back into things, despite her resistance. It had been a real struggle for him to get her to come on this trip at all.

"Maybe" was all she'd say about the circus.

When we got to Lascaux there was already a crowd waiting for the tours, which were led in several different languages. Our guide was a delicately boned girl wearing black leather pants that looked as if they'd been upholstered on her, and a tiny silver hoop through her eyebrow. I winced at the sight of it, though I'd seen plenty of them in Los Angeles and had almost gotten one myself. In the end I was too squeamish, and instead had extra holes pierced in each earlobe. The girl carried a large flashlight and spoke English with an adorable accent, unlike Stefan, whose pronunciation was flawless. I wondered why people with accents always sounded so charming, no matter what stupid or boring thing they said.

" 'Allo, welcome to Lascaux II, my name is Giselle," she said. "As you may know, this is a replica of the Lascaux cave, which is only several meters from here." She explained what Stefan had already told me, about why we couldn't see the real cave, and then went on. "The paintings you will see are around seventeen thousand years old. They are works of great art. *Great* art," she added, and nodded in emphasis.

It was cool and dim in the cave and even though I knew it was artificial, it felt quite real to me, especially so soon after my dream. We couldn't see much in the spectral dimness, and I wondered when Giselle was going to use her industrial-strength flashlight. She just stood quietly, waiting for us to settle down, to absorb the timeless sense of being inside the earth. Then she began to talk.

"The people who made the art of Lascaux were apparently as advanced as we are. It is believed they had art, religion, family life. They lived in a time of abundance because there were few people and many resources, which they used lightly. Unlike us."

There was a note of reproof in her voice. "They were wonderful problem solvers. They had to figure out how to do everything, you see. Make their own technology. They made specialized weapons and tools, which have been found buried with their dead. You know what that means?" She waited, but none of us said anything, even my father, who surely knew, or my mother, who always had an answer for everything.

"It means," she went on, "that they must have believed in an afterlife where the tools would be needed. This is a sophisticated concept, one that animals don't have. Also, my people made jewelry and carved designs on their tools and weapons, and painted on walls, so they were interested not only in survival but in beauty." Giselle really did seem well enough acquainted with these prehistoric people to consider them her own.

"There is no evidence that they ever lived in the cave of Lascaux. It is speculated that the cave's paintings had a religious purpose, but we do not know what that was. Hunting magic has been suggested, but I think no. This cave was for something grander, I feel it. There are other caves and shelters in this area where human habitation occurred, but those do not have painted walls.

"My people were clever in their art as well as so talented. They incorporated irregularities in the walls' surfaces into their paintings. A bulge in the wall became the shoulder of an aurochs. A dark horizontal line became the surface of water for swimming deer. To paint high on the walls, they built scaffolding. Clever, yes? You can see the holes where they wedged the framework. To see to work in the dark, they devised lamps of hollowed stone filled with fat, using wicks of braided vegetable fibers. They ground manganese and iron oxide and ochers to make pigment and, again cleverly, they stored these powders in hollowed and corked bird bones. Remember, this was before woven baskets, before ceramics—they had few containers."

Suddenly, behind my eyes flashed an image of hands filling these bone tubes, then fumbling among a litter of—I couldn't say what: stones, lumps of something—for the stoppers. It was gone in an instant, but it left an afterimage in my mind, like a photographic negative, and the sensation of reality. I shook my head, mystified and distracted, and tried to listen to Giselle.

"Though excellent animal figures abound, human figures are extremely rare in the art of the caves of the Dordogne. Yet my artists' skill was obviously equal to depicting them. Therefore, we speculate that there was some sort of taboo on realistic human portrayals. You will see this morning the single human figure from Lascaux. It is essentially a stick figure, not real and powerful as are the animals." She was silent, as if thinking. "Powerful," she said in a softer voice. "And now"—her voice rose again—"my favorite time. Pretend you are an artist, entering your cave to work on your masterpiece for your religion. You carry your tallow lamp with you, and the flame wavers on the wall, making it seem as if the animals there are moving, breathing, waiting for you. You enter with awe. With reverence." She clicked on her flashlight, but kept it pointed at her feet.

Gradually she raised the flashlight until it illuminated the cave wall—and an animal that looked like a cross between a horse and a bison, except that it had two long straight horns, very close together. She swept the flashlight quickly along one wall and back down the other wall of the corridor where we stood, and the initial, overwhelming impression I had was of being trapped in a stampede of big animals: deer and bison, horses and cows. They were crowded together, sometimes overlapping, large and strong, filled with a sense of life and movement that was emphasized by the way Giselle moved the flashlight.

A shiver ran up my backbone and I had another of those strange picture-flashes inside my head: a herd of red deer was running across my field of vision, partly obscured by the leaves of the bush I crouched behind. I was sure I could feel the earth tremble under the animals' hooves.

I reached for my father's arm. "Are we having an earthquake?" I whispered in his ear.

He looked down at me, his eyes concerned behind his glasses. "No. Are you dizzy? Is it the dark?"

Giselle was giving us a silencing look, so I just shook my head at him, but I held on to his arm. As it turned out, that was a good thing, because the more we explored the cave in the dark, looking at the wonderfully alive animals shifting with the changing light, charging along over our heads, the dizzier I felt. I was sure the ground was vibrating with their running. I could swear I smelled them, gamey and sharp.

I held more tightly to my father, but in spite of that, I felt alone with the animals, so sure was I that no one else knew them as I did, as living embodiments of power and importance from the artists' time.

I missed a lot of what Giselle was saying. I was so overcome by the sensation of breathing animals around me, rushing past me, of deep echoes of complex life, that it took me a while to recognize something else I was feeling—an unquiet sense of familiarity, as if this wasn't the first time I'd seen these paintings. Of course, I'd seen pictures in my father's books, but what I felt was almost that I'd *been* here before.

My father kept his hand over mine where I clutched his shirt sleeve, until we left the cave and returned to the blinding glare of the world outside. "Are you all right?" he asked as we walked to the car. "What happened in there?"

"I don't know," I said. Already the dark cave with its sense of living presences seemed remote and incredible. "I felt like—I know this sounds crazy—but I felt like the animals were alive."

"You've always had a vivid imagination," my mother said, her beautiful voice making her words sound like a compliment, when I knew she didn't mean them to be.

"They were wonderfully realistic," my father said, still holding on to me. "And the lighting was pretty spooky. Giselle had a way of re-creating the atmosphere, didn't she?" I had made excuses for his not knowing who Jay Leno and Jerry Seinfeld were, and now he was going to find an explanation for my reaction to the cave art. "The way she acted out the thoughts of the artist was remarkable."

"She did what?"

"Don't you remember how she pretended she was the artist coming into the cave, seeing the white calcite surfaces and speculating what he—or maybe she— would make there?"

"A little, I guess."

"She said the work was so fine that the artists—perhaps a master and his students—had to have practiced in other places, too, perhaps in this same area. Lascaux was found by some boys chasing their dog down a hole. It's possible that there are other caves as wonderful, waiting to be found as simply."

I didn't remember any of that. My mind had been too full of thundering animals and a sense of the artists' presence. Maybe my mother was right; maybe I did have too vivid an imagination.

"I think you must have been overstimulated in there," my father said. "I'm sure you'll feel better after some lunch and a rest."

I remembered Stefan. "Actually," I said, "I'm going to have lunch with someone from the circus. And he's going to take me for a canoe ride on the river."

"From the circus?" my mother asked incredulously.

"It's not the same as an asylum," I answered tartly. "I met him yesterday. He's a clown. And a juggler," I added, as if that would impress my mother.

"Are you sure he's all right?" my father asked more mildly. "You don't know anything about him, and you know how circus people—" He stopped, watching me carefully. "They *are* Gypsies," he said.

"Gypsies!" my mother cried. "Oh, really, Hannah. Really!"

"It's just a picnic, for pete's sake," I said. "He's bringing the piglet he uses in his act. Does that sound like he's a dangerous guy? If he gets fresh I promise I'll scream my head off and kick him in the—in the piglet and run for my life."

My mother opened her mouth, but Dad put his hand on her arm and she closed it. "Well, Mother and I will be having lunch in the hotel if you change your mind."

Fat chance of that, I thought.

Seven

The back of my shirt was sticking to me when I approached the circus tent, and my bangs were wet on my forehead.

A line of horses stood tethered in the meadow, flicking at flies with their tails while they cropped the high grass with big yellow teeth. Babette, a chain around one of her rear legs, played in a tub of water, splashing herself with her trunk.

Several motor homes were parked to the side of the tent, and beside them dark-haired people sat in lawn chairs, talking. A man trimmed the hair of a boy sitting between his knees; a woman with a braid down to her waist knitted; a boy about Stefan's age wrapped tape around the handle of an implement I didn't recognize.

As I approached, they stopped talking and watched me. Even the little children stopped playing and stared, some of them going to cling to their mothers' knees. I felt self-conscious, afraid to violate some Gypsy etiquette by going closer.

Stefan came through the door of one of the motor homes, Fifi under one arm and the string bag over his shoulder. He said some words in Romany, and the adults seemed to relax slightly, though the children stayed at their mothers' sides.

A man in a sleeveless T-shirt, his bulky shoulder muscles flexing as he pushed himself from his lawn chair, spoke to me in accented English. "You enjoyed our performance last night?"

I didn't recognize him from the night before, but I said, "Yes, very much." When he didn't speak again, I added, "You were all wonderful."

"I am Ivor Kremo, Stefan's father," he said.

"Hannah Flood. Nice to meet you." I extended my hand.

He inclined his dark head, but didn't take my hand, which I withdrew awkwardly. Maybe shaking hands wasn't a Gypsy custom. Or maybe they just didn't shake hands with—what had Stefan said?—*gadje.*

By this time Stefan was beside me. He put Fifi on the ground and handed me her leash. He spoke in Romany to his father, who answered him, sounding displeased. They exchanged a few more words and then Stefan turned to leave, pushing me ahead of him. We hadn't gone far before I heard behind us an adolescent voice calling something and making a noise I didn't know the meaning of but which sounded rude.

Stefan turned, yelled something, and turned back. "My cousin Lucien thinks he's very smart," he said.

When we were out of earshot, I said, "Did I offend your family somehow? They seemed so . . . I don't know . . . restrained." I put it as politely as I could.

"Because you're *gadje. Gadje* in bunches, like the circus audiences, are one thing. A single female *gadji* with a Rom man is another. They don't like it. Especially after Ka . . . my brother.''

He'd given me an opening I couldn't resist. ''What happened to your brother?''

Stefan sighed and walked a little before he spoke. ''He left the circus. With a *gadji* from Paris.'' He watched his feet taking steps along the dirt lane.

''But doesn't that make him''—I searched for the word—*''merimay?''*

He nodded. ''He's more than dead to them.''

Maybe he was more than dead to the rest of the family, but I could tell he wasn't to Stefan.

''Do you know where he is now? Is he still with her?''

''He's in Paris. But not with her. She was just his way out, his excuse. He's working for IBM, waiting for a transfer to the States.''

So Stefan's brother had studied the universal languages of numbers and computers, too. No wonder no one in Le Cirque d'Été had been glad to see me. And, clearly, Stefan had been in touch with the outcast.

''You must miss him,'' I said carefully, stopping to let Fifi sniff at something interesting in the weeds beside the path.

''Yes,'' he said, his voice soft. Then he took a breath and said, ''So tell me how was Lascaux. Did you like it?''

''I liked it too much, I think.''

''What do you mean?'' He turned to look at me.

''I had the strangest sensation in there. As if I'd been there before. And as if the animals were alive. I thought I could smell them and feel the heat from their bodies, and the ground shake when they ran by. I even had a couple of—I don't know what to call them, flashbacks

· 45 ·

or hallucinations or something; I was seeing things that weren't there." I gave an embarrassed laugh and added, "I must still have jet lag."

"Maybe not," Stefan said. "Has anything like this ever happened to you before?"

"Of course not."

"Hey," he said, "remember I am a Rom. We believe in the Sight. Such experiences are not so strange to us."

"The Sight?"

"You know, the ability to see what isn't there, to receive signals from some other plane, to understand what others cannot."

"Maybe just Gypsies have that."

"No. *Gadje* do, too. But for some reason it is easier for Travelers to believe in the Sight than for others. Yet the Sight doesn't care who believes in it; it is still there."

In spite of the bright day, the hot summer sunshine, I sensed a film of something dark almost at the edge of my vision. Something unknown but not menacing. Something big and alive and real.

"Have you ever experienced . . . the Sight?"

"Yes." He was solemn, respectful. "Many times. Once I dreamed my brother fell from the high wire. I told no one because I didn't want to suggest it to him. The mind can be a powerful thing, you know. Ten days later he fell. Exactly as he had in my dream, with a balancing cane in his hand, wearing his white tights with the silver stripes."

I waited.

"He hit the net, but he hit it wrong and broke his shoulder. The same as in my dream."

In my pragmatic opinion, it wasn't the Sight that accounted for dreaming about falls when you were a tightrope artist.

"I could have warned him," Stefan added. "He might have been prepared if I had warned him."

"No one can be prepared for a fall," I said. "You thought you were doing the right thing." But I recognized his guilt, that obsessive need to go back over the events, to try to muscle them into a different ending, to feel responsible somehow for the outcome. What if Mark and I had doubled with Molly and Peter to the New Year's Eve party? Then they'd have left at a different time, with us, and avoided the drunk driver. But I'd wanted to be alone with Mark, to drink champagne and kiss him in the dark, and I hadn't wanted to go home when Molly and Peter did, at a sensible hour. If I hadn't been so selfish, so pleasure-centered, so self-indulgent, I'd have been able to save Molly. It made sense to me.

"So the Sight isn't a good thing?" I asked.

"It's not good or bad. It just is. Just as my brother's fate is his own."

We reached the poplar trees beside the river and stepped gratefully into their shade. Stefan opened the string bag and spread out a clean blue-checked cloth for us to sit on. He fastened Fifi's leash to a length of rope and tied the rope's end around a tree so she could wander a bit.

"And where is your sister?" he asked, lying back on the picnic cloth, his strong hands clasped behind his head. "The one with the graceful genes."

I hadn't talked to anyone about Molly in the last six months—not my parents, not my friends. She'd only gone round and round in my own head while I was awake and while I slept. "She's . . . gone. You know. Passed on. Departed."

"Ah," Stefan said, finally understanding. "How?"

"A drunk driver. New Year's Eve. She and her boy-friend both."

"I'm sorry. How old was she?"

"She was my twin."

He sat up, clasping his arms around his raised knees, and slowly shook his head, murmuring something in Romany.

"I haven't cried for her," I said. "Not one tear."

"You will," he said. "When it happens, don't be afraid. You have to do it."

He sounded as if he knew what he was talking about, but I didn't believe it would ever happen to me. "If I have tears, they're frozen into an ice block so big and hard it'll never thaw."

Talking about Molly seemed to freshen the sense of loss that on its best days was an aching dullness, and on its worst an excruciating amputation. In some ways, I missed her more now than I had at first. I'd gotten over the feeling I had the first two or three months that this was temporary, that I could say, "Okay, the joke's over. Now come on back, Molly." I was seventeen now, about to be a senior, and she never would be. I'd been to France, and she hadn't. And she knew the answer to the ultimate mystery, and I didn't.

Stefan said, *"Feri ando payi sitsholpe te noyuas."*

"What's that?" I asked.

"A Rom saying. We have lots of sayings, most of which can be interpreted in more than one way. This one means, 'It is in the water that one learns to swim.'"

"I don't get it."

"Once you're in the water, even if it's not your idea to be there, you have two choices: you can drown or you can swim. Which is yours?"

I thought. "I feel like I'm drowning, but I'm still here, so I must be swimming, even if not very well."

"I'm swimming, too," he said.

"My sister was named Molly," I said. "What is your brother's name?" I asked. "Can you tell me?"

He was silent so long I wondered if he'd heard me. And then he said, "Karel. His name is Karel." He rolled over and rummaged in the string bag. "How about some lunch?"

"Sure."

Stefan handed me a paper plate with a chicken leg, a bunch of grapes, a chunk of French bread, and three little tomatoes. He opened a bottle of water and removed the cork from a half-drunk bottle of red wine. He poured a glass of wine and handed it to me.

"No, thanks," I said. "I don't drink anymore."

"Ah," he said, "the drunk driver." He poured water for me instead and added some to his wine. "I don't like it full-strength. The French, they think this is horrible, to dilute good wine." He shrugged. "That's how I like it."

As we ate, I remembered my dream. It may have been because I was still thinking about the Sight that I mentioned it to Stefan.

He sat up and wiped his fingers on a paper napkin. "This is interesting," he said. "You dream of a cave before you go to see one. You dream of collecting bones for burning. Did you know that prehistoric people used to do that when there was no wood? No? Are you sure?" I shook my head again. "Did you know that in the real cave of Lascaux, but not reproduced in Lascaux II, there is what they call the Chamber of the Felines, where there are drawings and etchings of lions? It's at the end of a long passage, well away from the other animals, as if to keep the lions hidden there, where they can do no harm."

I felt chilly fingertips along my spine. "Really?" Had my father mentioned this fact and my subconscious somehow remembered?

"Really. Of course, no one knows what purpose the cave served, so no one knows why the lions are so hidden away. In other caves this is true, too; the lions are in far chambers, along with the bears and the rhinos. The carnivores, the most dangerous creatures. Interesting, isn't it?"

"How come you know so much about these caves?" I asked.

"The mystery interests me. Perhaps because my origins are mysterious, too. No one is entirely sure about the source of the Travelers. And also because we Roma have our own secrets that make sense to us but not to *gadje*. We're outsiders by history and by preference." He gave me his buccaneer's grin.

I wondered why he had befriended me so easily when he had so many family members to spend time with.

"So now you're wondering why I come on a picnic with you," he said, "when my family disapproves." I stared at him. He laughed at my look. "No, that was not the Sight. It's a natural thing to wonder." He shrugged. "It happens now and then. I meet someone in a town where we're playing. There's something about her that connects with me somehow. Who can explain attraction and rapport? Perhaps it comes from a time when we knew each other as Unborn Souls. I felt that with you. Perhaps you were Roma in a life before this one. It is said, you know, that we return with those we have known in other lives, to continue to work out our business with them.''

The idea appealed to me. I knew my mother the scientist would ridicule such thoughts, but I liked thinking that Stefan and I were resuming a friendship begun in another life. That Molly and I could be together again somewhere.

"Maybe," I said. "Anything's possible, I suppose."

Eight

Fifi finished the chicken Stefan had cut up for her and came to snuffle at our plates. Stefan picked her up and hugged her until she squealed, and then gave her more chicken bits, feeding them to her from his fingers. She took the chicken delicately in her mouth and looked up at him with adoring eyes. "Fifi, my love, your manners are exquisite," he said, and goggled adoringly back at her. We both laughed, and Fifi made a little snorting sound.

Stefan reached into the string bag and took out five red rubber balls. "This time you juggle with balls, not plums," he said to me. "Far less messy."

So we had another lesson, and I was better than I had been the day before. I got three balls into the air, at least for a little while, and paid attention as Stefan demonstrated the Cascade and the Shower and the Double Shower, techniques that I could aspire to. Then he made me practice some more.

After twenty minutes, with all the balls on the ground

and Fifi chasing after them, I wailed, "Oh, I wish they *were* plums. Then they'd all be smashed and I could quit this."

I wanted juggling to come easily, and if it didn't, well, forget it. But I envied Stefan's dedication, his goal to juggle nine balls, his passion for something outside himself. I hoped I'd find my own someday, something to pull me from the darkness inside my head.

"Then we're finished," Stefan said, picking up four balls and leaving one for Fifi to push around. "It's not supposed to be torture."

"I don't mean to hurt your feelings," I said.

He looked at me, surprised. "Why should my feelings be hurt? This isn't what you want to do. It *is* what I want to do, that's all."

"I suppose the Travelers have a saying for that, too," I said sourly.

"You suppose correctly," he said, scaling the balls up into a parabola over his head. "Let's see if I can think of one. Ah, this might do. *Yekka buliasa nashti beshes pe done grastende.* 'With one behind you cannot sit on two horses.' "

"What?" I fell over laughing, and Fifi pushed her ball up to my face, grunting.

Stefan laughed, too, but his hands stayed steady and the red balls remained in the air. "Now let me see if I can think of a sensible way to interpret this one. How's this? You can't keep trying to do too many things at once, especially things you don't want to do."

"Oh, I get it," I said, rolling Fifi's ball for her. "It just sounds so funny."

"It would be a good circus saying even if it wasn't a Roma one. Come on, let's go get a canoe."

I sat up. "Can Fifi go in a canoe with us?"

"She loves it. Wait and see."

Stefan was right. After we rented a canoe from the dock in town, he put the cloth from our picnic in the bottom of it. Fifi stepped daintily onto the cloth and sat down. Before we set off into the river, Stefan handed me a bottle of sunblock and told me to rub some on Fifi. A pig's skin is sensitive to sun, and Fifi was just a baby. She loved it, rolling over so I could get to her tummy and giving me her silly piggy grin.

Stefan pushed us out into the current and maneuvered the canoe around with the paddles. Where we were, the river was slow, almost indolent, and we could drift without any effort. I sat in the bottom of the boat with Fifi curled beside me, asleep, and closed my eyes.

Behind them flashed a picture of hands over water, hands with a spear, taking aim at a big fish idling in the shade of the overhanging rock. I jerked my eyes open and sat up straight.

"What?" Stefan asked.

"I just had one of those prehistoric hallucinations or whatever they are. I saw hands with a spear aiming for a fish in the water."

"Many primitive tribes still fish that way, even though it's not as efficient as net fishing. It calls for more personal skill. Of course, that's the way the people who lived in this area had to fish before they invented nets."

"I think I must be suffering some kind of hysteria from seeing Lascaux, don't you?"

"I think you are Seeing," he said easily. "With the Sight."

"Oh, don't say that. It scares me."

"Why?" he said. "Aren't we each the product of all

our accumulated experiences? It's not so hard for me to consider that some of those experiences came from lives we've lived before this one."

I was cold even in the sun. "I don't know if I believe in reincarnation. It seems so farfetched."

"It does? A lot of religions believe in it. And so do many people who aren't religious. How can you explain Mozart, who was composing minuets at five, or those kids who program computers at four or are in college by the time they're ten? How do you explain those feelings of déjà vu that we all get?"

"I don't know, but I'm sure my mother would have an explanation. She's a scientist and *everything* has a scientific explanation, whether it's UFOs or Elvis sightings or déjà vu."

He lifted one shoulder and one eyebrow. "Your mother could be wrong."

"I often think so. About a lot of things."

"You see?" he said. "So why shouldn't you remember something from long ago when you're in the place where it happened?"

I shook my head. "I'm sorry. I can't get my mind around that."

"You know, the psychologist Carl Jung believed in the collective unconscious, a sort of race memory we all share of experiences that haven't happened to us directly but to previous humans."

"Where do you get all this stuff? I've been trudging through school for eleven years and this is all news to me."

"I've had to educate myself, so I read what interests me. I guess I know a lot of what might seem peculiar to you. I can't diagram sentences or explain the circulatory system, the way you probably can, but I doubt I'll ever need to.''

"I doubt I'll ever need to, either. Some of those things you know seem like a more interesting way to fill up my head.''

The canoe entered an eddy and swung around and around in a slow circle, repeating what my mind was doing. Fifi snorted in her sleep and rearranged herself on the picnic cloth.

Stefan stuck the paddle into the water, breaking our pattern and sending us out into the current again.

"I'm probably just impressionable,'' I said. "Since Molly's been . . . gone, my brain hasn't worked the way it used to. I feel like there's a short circuit somewhere that makes it hard for me to think straight.''

"Whatever you say,'' Stefan said absently. But I knew I wasn't going to get his ideas out of my thoughts so easily. And somehow I liked the prospect of having them to turn and weigh, to occupy my mind, which needed something besides sorrow on it.

"Are you coming to the performance tonight?'' he asked. "You can be my guest again.''

"I'd like to. I think my father wants to come, too.''

"What about your mother?''

"I don't know. She's resisting.''

"I'll give you three tickets. Maybe that will make the choice easier for her.''

"That's very generous. You don't have to do that.''

"I know.'' Placidly he dipped the oars, moving us from the middle of the river to the bank and back again. There were no other craft on the water, though we could see people on the shore, working in the fields or hanging laundry on back-yard lines. Almost all of them waved as we drifted by, as if they were friendly natives in a public television travelogue.

I closed my eyes and drowsed again, the top of my head feeling scorched by the sun. The bump of the canoe against the downriver dock brought me out of a satisfying semi-trance occupied entirely by Stefan: his lively mind, his humor, his pain over Karel. And, equally important, his beautiful eyes, his muscular arms, his exotic allure. A part of myself I thought permanently dormant seemed to be waking up, too.

We were helped from the canoe by a surly sunburned teenage boy who shuttled us in a rattly truck back to where we started. He responded to Stefan's attempts at conversation with grunts, and I thought he'd have been a better companion for Fifi than he was for us.

At the dock where we'd rented our canoe, we collected the string bag and started back toward the village. Before we parted at the lane where Stefan would return to the circus, he handed me three tickets for that evening's performance.

"No flowers tonight, okay?" I asked.

"You didn't like them?" he asked.

"You know I did. But my mother might be there. Sometimes she overreacts." I could just imagine what she'd say about a Gypsy circus clown giving me flowers.

"Okay," he said, unperturbed. "Tonight will be something different."

"Oh, no. What?"

He smiled and turned his back, leading Fifi away with him. She turned to look back at me and then sat down in the dusty lane, resisting Stefan's tugging.

"I think she wants to say goodbye to me. Or au revoir. What language does she speak?"

"Pig Latin, what else?" he said, laughing.

He brought her back, and I knelt to hug her. She put her little trotters up on my knees and pushed her nose into my cheek. I could have sworn she was giving me a kiss, and the sweetness of the gesture made me feel the stupid helpless prickling of tears behind my eyes. I couldn't cry when Molly died, but I could when a pig kissed me.

Still on my knees, I watched Stefan and Fifi go off down the path. I took a couple of long, deep, noisy sniffs and got up.

Nine

At dinner I showed my parents the circus tickets and Dad said, "In this case, Mother, you have to go. It would be rude not to. And don't you want to meet Hannah's clown?"

"Well, of course I'm dying to meet Hannah's clown," my mother said, making even sarcasm sound like music. "But I'll have to change into something more . . . circusy."

"How about something with sequins and plumes?" I said. "That should do it."

She gave me a long expressionless look and then said, "I meant slacks and walking shoes."

Once again I was in the front row, this time with my parents. And this time I could pick Stefan out of the parade, even though his clown costume was somewhat different than it had been the night before. He was leading Fifi, who wore a pointed pink hat with a big heart-shaped pom-pom on the top.

He juggled his rings. He did his act with the bubbles, which delighted my father as much as it did every child in the audience, though my mother seemed unimpressed, unengaged. Stefan's high-wire act was, if anything, more daring than the night before, and his fall into the net scared me more than it had then, since now I knew about the fall that had broken his brother's shoulder.

His final appearance was with Fifi again, but this time he carried a basket from which he gave her treats. Then he took from the basket a red satin heart and put it into her mouth. She trotted with it straight to me and laid it at my feet. Then she scampered back to Stefan, who handed her another heart. She repeated the delivery of a heart seven times more, while the older members of the audience whistled and the children laughed. If I'd been embarrassed by the flowers, this was even worse.

"Your clown seems serious," Dad said.

"It's just part of his act," I said, hoping I sounded matter-of-fact. Thinking it would help me get over my embarrassment, I decided to become part of the act. I blew kisses to Stefan, who pretended to faint with joy. Fifi hovered over him, and the children screamed for him to get up. He did, patting his heart with his big white gloves and beaming shyly. This time he handed Fifi the whole basket, and with a tremendous effort, which had the audience shouting encouragement to her, she dragged it over to me, spilling out the remaining hearts at my feet. I took one, hugged it, and tossed it to Stefan.

He did a whole number with it—gazing at it, amazed, looking bashfully in my direction, showing it to Fifi, to the audience, hugging it.

I threw him another and he went through the same routine. Then I sailed hearts, one after another, at him as fast as he could catch them. He piled them before him, acting as thrilled as if he'd found buried treasure. When he had all the hearts back again, he bent to tie one to Fifi's collar and then threw all but two, a big one and a tiny one, into the audience. Children and adults both scrambled to catch the hearts, as if they really contained all the love Stefan had been pantomiming.

He tucked the little heart inside his long underwear, patting it into place over his chest. Then, taking Fifi's leash, he walked all the way around the ring, carrying the big heart, until he came to me. Squirming and lowering his eyes in embarrassment, he laid the heart in my lap. Then he bolted from the tent, with Fifi under his arm and his big shoes flapping.

The audience burst into cheers, craning to look at me and shouting out what I took to be romantic advice.

"These French!" my father said into my ear. "Always interested in *l'amour*. There's a note pinned to your pillow," he added.

I opened it carefully so that neither of my parents could see what was written there. It said: *Wait for me after the show. S.*

As if I needed to be invited. All the circus horses in France couldn't have made me leave until I'd seen him.

"He wants me to wait for him," I said. "You two can go on back to the hotel. I'll come along later."

"I don't think that's a very good idea," my mother said.

"Why not?" I asked. "I can find my way home. I did it last night and you didn't worry then."

"Your judgment, which has sometimes been questionable, isn't at its best now," my mother said. "This—this boy could be dangerous to you in a deserted circus tent."

"It won't be deserted," I said, bristling at her remark about my judgment. "It takes a long time to clean it up. Besides, I was alone with him all afternoon on a deserted river. I don't see the difference." I could never tell if my mother was really concerned for my welfare or if she was just trying to make things hard for me.

"She'll be all right," Dad said, standing and taking my mother's elbow.

I appreciated his recent efforts to be less protective. He understood, if my mother didn't, that no matter how strenuously they tried to safeguard me, Molly would still be gone.

"Alex, I don't think—" she began, but he gently pulled her to her feet.

"Don't be too late," he said, and led her away.

She didn't go easily. I could see her trying to get her arm out of my father's grip, could hear her: "This is irresponsible and dangerous and I don't see how you can condone such a thing. How can you be so careless?" she went on, furious and frustrated.

"It'll be all right," my father kept saying until I couldn't hear him anymore. He was promising her something we had to believe to keep living. My mother wanted us to be stored safely away, protected forever, and my father knew we couldn't live like that. At least Molly had died doing something she was enjoying.

Once they were gone, I felt more like my old self than I had in a long time, full of curiosity and excitement. Okay, so my judgment wasn't always great. I was a kid, for heaven's sake. I was learning. Was I supposed to be perfect, the way my mother thought Molly was?

I knew Molly wasn't perfect. For all her virtues, she was a total slob, with dirty dishes under her bed and a hairbrush so tangled with hair she could hardly use it. But my mother considered these harmless foibles, while *my* faults, she believed, held potential for disaster.

Stefan returned, this time without Fifi, in his jeans and a University of Tasmania sweatshirt. His hair was wet and showed the comb tracks. "Hi," he said. "You want to join the circus? The crowd loved it when you threw those pillows back at me."

"I only did it because I don't have room in my luggage for them. It's already full of flowers."

"Did I embarrass you?"

"Just for a minute. Then it was fun."

"You look nice," he said. "We should go somewhere with you all dressed up like that."

"Don't you have to help clean up?"

"Not tonight."

"Where can we go?"

"I'll buy you an espresso at the bistro in town. Okay?"

"Great." I was thinking my mother should hear this. Pretty risky goings-on.

So we had coffee and talked. And when I walked him back to the lane where he would leave me to return to Le Cirque d'Été, he kissed me good night. Or I kissed him. The idea seemed to occur to both of us at the same time. And a wonderful idea it was, too. Wonderful enough to really give my mother something to worry about. Wonderful enough to rekindle my guilt at having such pleasure.

On the way to the hotel, I wondered what my dreams, so predictable until last night, would be about tonight. I was way overdue for a dream about something marvelous.

Ten

For a long time, there was only pain and the shriek of the storm wind. Then there was cold and hunger, and more pain.

There were voices that she recognized: her mother, her sister, the others of the family. Mai, her sister, stayed closest, and she knew why. It was the sister's duty to receive the dying one's last breath. She would welcome death, she longed for it as relief from the pain of the lion.

There was darkness and the smell of bodies, and smoke and fear. And then the pain was less, and there was quiet and more light.

She could hear Mother's voice singing to Earth-the-Mother; first, the thanking song for her daughter's surviving the lion, then the blessing song, and finally the asking song, asking for meat.

There had been no meat when she set out to look for firewood and there still was none, who knew how much later.

Sleep again, and lessening pain and growing hunger. She

opened her eyes. "Go to the lion's cave," she said. "He will be our meat."

Even with her eyes closed, she could visualize, from the sounds she heard, the family gathering their spears and sharp flint knives for skinning and butchering, their skin carrying bags and tying thongs.

Sleep was the best escape from cold and pain and hunger.

When she woke, the skin shelter was bright with firelight, and the air was rich with the smell of cooking meat and dripping fat. They had saved the liver for her, the strongest part, the hunter's reward. Now she would carry the lion with her forever, not only in her memory and her scars, but as a part of her. He had both maimed her and saved her.

After that, the spring came quickly, with the sound of melting, running water and the smell of damp earth and new green growth.

Then they were on their way to the summer grounds, to meet with the other families, to have the initiation ceremony, arrange the year's marriages, hunt, and preserve food for the winter, which always returned. Mai would be married this summer, she was sure of it, but she herself would not. And with the terrible, disfiguring scars from the cave lion's fangs and claws, she probably never would be anyone's wife. The summer, which she'd always looked forward to and loved, loomed now as a time of loss and farewell: to Mai, who would go with her new family at summer's end; to her own future, which was forever changed; to everything familiar from the past.

She was tired of the looks on the faces of everyone who saw her scars, the horror and the pity and sometimes the relief that it was her and not them. She was tired of explaining.

It was quiet down by the river, where she could pretend to be spearfishing.

She jumped when she heard her name.

"An-Nay," Mother said, "what are you doing here? You must help me, you know."

"I can grind the pigments and make the crayons," she said, "but I can't go into the cave. I'm too ugly to enter the beautiful cave, and besides, now I'm afraid of caves."

"Nonsense," Mother said. "The purpose of the cave is to teach you how to be, not how to look. And you are a good artist, too good to waste when we need so much help. Come."
She held out her hand.

"I can't. Give me the pigments and the fat. I'll grind colors and make crayons."

"For now, then," Mother said. "But only for now."

Alone again, she closed her eyes against the heavy sun and remembered other caves, ceremonial caves that she'd been unafraid to enter: the narrow, twisting entrances, the passages of rebirth. The chambers filled with animal spirits waiting to infuse the boys about to become men. Bison, big, shaggy, and nimble. Deer, a good swimmer, with acute senses. Cow, patient and thoughtful. Aurochs, strong and clever. Reindeer, whose every part was useful in some way. Only the strongest, surest, most important animals were there on the walls to inspire the boys to become what they needed to be. And the hidden Chamber of the Carnivores was always there, too, to remind the boys of traits to guard against: viciousness, treachery, selfishness.

She shivered at the thought of the lions in the Chamber of the Carnivores, and tried to turn her thoughts in a more positive direction.

But there didn't seem to be one. She couldn't be an artist if

*she was afraid to enter a cave. She would never be a wife.
And worst of all, Mai, the companion of every day she had
lived, would leave her soon.*

*She wished she could drown her despair, throw it into the
sunstruck water, to let it swirl and eddy and drift away from
her.*

Eleven

I lay in that liquid limbo between sleep and waking where everything seemed real and possible. I felt the smile on my face, knowing it came from a combination of the memory of Stefan's kiss and the memory of a dream that seemed still tucked mistily into the crevices of my mind. It was the first time in six months that the void left by Molly wasn't my first thought on waking.

I had dreamed about a lost time again, and again it had seemed so real. I could almost feel the wounds and scars of the cave lion on my own body; feel the fear of the cave, as well as the awe and reverence for it. And I could certainly identify with the girl, An-Nay's, dread of her sister's loss. But in the dream the sister was still there. Perhaps there was a way the loss could be prevented or postponed.

Well, why shouldn't a dream seem real to me? My own life didn't. Hadn't since New Year's Eve. Molly's death had catapulted me from my familiar life into what seemed like another universe where everything looked the same but was completely different, where my old interests held no attraction, my friends couldn't talk to me, my emotions were dim memories. Coming to the Dordogne seemed to have brought me to earth again, where I was having picnics with a Gypsy clown and a pig named Fifi, juggling plums, and going to the circus every night. In the past six months I'd forgotten that I was the kind of person who liked doing such uncommon and happy things.

I opened my eyes to a room flooded with sunlight. I'd left the curtains open the night before so I could watch the moon shine in on the cabbage roses and the paper ones and the real ones in my room, hoping the sight would sweeten my dreams. Apparently it had.

Dad and I met in the dining room for breakfast; Mother, as usual, was sleeping in.

"I thought today we could go to one of the other caves," Dad said as he buttered a croissant. "There's Font-de-Gaume or Les Combarelles, or maybe Laugerie Haute, which isn't a cave but more of a shelter, a kind of rock overhang called an *abri*, where the early people lived. Are you interested?"

"If we could go this morning. I have sort of a picnic date for lunch."

"Ah," Dad said. He stopped buttering his croissant and looked down at it in his hand. I waited for him to say something about how I should be careful, how Gypsies weren't to be trusted, how I hardly knew this boy. But he didn't say it. He put the buttered croissant in his mouth, instead. After he'd chewed it, he said, "All right. I'll have the concierge call ahead and see if there are tickets available. Which would you like to see?"

"I've seen a cave. How about the shelter? It would be interesting to imagine how they lived." In truth, I could more than imagine it. I could see it, a relic from my dream: a skin tent erected inside the *abri* during the winter, camps and cooking fires by the river in the summer. I wasn't as curious as I should have been, and when Dad returned from his phone calls, I wasn't really disappointed to hear that the only tickets still available were for the afternoon tours.

"Maybe Mother will go with you again," I said.

"I'll ask her," he said. "Are you sure you don't want to come? This is such a magical area, you shouldn't miss any of the extraordinary sights."

Dad, in typical professorial style, thought he could transfer to me the fixation he'd had since boyhood. But I seemed to have found my own fascination, if my dreams were any indication, and my own magic relationship with this place.

"I don't want *you* to miss anything, Dad. So don't wait for me. Or for Mother, either, if she isn't interested. You go."

He drank his coffee. "You're right, I will. What will you do until lunchtime?"

"I don't know. I might sit in the sun and read. Or take a walk. Don't worry about me. I'll be fine."

"You . . ." he began and then stopped. "Okay. I'll see you later, then." He left the table, stopping once to look back at me as I drank my chocolate. I waved.

My mother ended up going with him, but not without the usual coaxing. After they left, I felt as if a suffocating cloud had lifted. To know that they were somewhere else, doing something that had no connection with me, made me feel as light and free as the golden, scented air outside.

I finished my chocolate and went upstairs. The maid had already made up my room and I drifted around it, touching surfaces, fingering my satin heart and my paper flowers, looking out the window, willing the time to pass, to become noon.

I went into my parents' room looking for the guidebook, hoping Dad hadn't taken it with him. I found it on the bedside table and sat on his bed, riffling through the pages, finding the section on the caves. It didn't tell me anything I hadn't already heard from Stefan or Giselle. I replaced the book and on impulse, thinking there might be some tourist brochures there, opened the drawer in the table between the two beds. Looking up at me from a small silver frame was a picture of Molly. I knew it was Molly and not me because of the hairstyle and the tiny scar over her eyebrow that she'd gotten falling off her tricycle.

I rose and went to the bureau, where I knew only my mother's things would be arranged. She was too organized to live out of a suitcase if we stayed more than one night in a place. My father had appropriated the luggage rack for his opened suitcase and a chair for everything else and somehow managed to find whatever he needed in the mess he'd made.

In my mother's drawer was an envelope with photographs of Molly: not with any of her friends or with me, just her alone. There, too, was Molly's charm bracelet and a three-inch Stieff teddy bear that Molly had taken everywhere with her when she was little and later had kept on her nightstand.

The pictures of Molly seemed to taunt me with her loss. I'd removed all her photos from my bulletin board the day of her funeral, wondering if I'd be able ever to put them up again.

I wondered whether my mother would have brought reminders of me, if it had been me instead of Molly who died. I didn't like having to wonder.

Back in my own room, I watched the hands on the clock until finally they moved close to noon. I brushed my hair and left to meet Stefan.

He and Fifi were waiting for me on the path between the circus tent and the village. He handed me Fifi's leash, and we went off along the path that now seemed as familiar as if I'd been walking it all my life.

"I'll miss this town," Stefan said. "Most of them I forget, but not this one."

"Why not?" I asked. Fifi had stopped to root at something and I stood, waiting.

"Because here I met you." He stopped beside me and put his hand on the back of my neck. I closed my eyes.

"I wonder how long you'll remember me," I said, almost in a whisper.

"Why, always," he said, sounding surprised. "Always. You are a part of who I become. You are in me now, forever."

I wanted more. "But everybody you meet is part of who you become, part of the sum of your experiences. Why don't you remember them all?"

"Because not all of them add to what I am. You do." He moved his hand on the back of my neck. Fifi continued to snuffle in the weeds. "You won't forget me, either," he said.

He was definitely right about that. Suddenly Fifi was finished with her exploration and trotted ahead on the path, pulling her leash taut. I opened my eyes and followed her. Stefan's hand dropped from my neck.

"The truck's fixed, isn't it?" I asked.

"It will be by this evening. We'll leave after the performance, early in the morning, while it's still dark."

"And I'll never see you again," I said.

"We can't know that," he said. "The future holds its mysteries. But even if that's so, I'll go with you in your mind."

"It's not enough," I said, furious. I didn't want one more lost person to carry in my mind. I wanted real people, ones who would stay with me, would be there in more than memory.

"It's what we have," he said. "We have a saying—"

"I knew it."

"—that goes, 'A candle is not made of wax but is all flame.' That's how we are now."

"I'd make a terrible Traveler. I don't understand any of these sayings."

"I know you understand this one. The flame is what makes the candle what it is, the flame is the existence. The flame is the *now*. That's all any of us have. We can't know the future or even if there is to be one. We must concentrate on being the flame."

"It's not enough," I said again, stubbornly. This flame business might be true, but it was very little comfort.

"It's what we have." He stopped, set down the string bag, and put his arms around me. We stood in the shade of a walnut tree with Fifi, in a hurry now, pulling on her leash while he kissed me with kisses more expressive than I could have thought possible. There was love and loss and tenderness and comfort and a shade of anger in them, and I knew he felt as I did, that he hated having to say goodbye to one more person. But that was the way it was going to be with us, and there was nothing we could do about it except learn to be the flame instead of the candle.

Fifi was squealing now in her hurry to get going, and Stefan and I came apart, laughing at her. We walked on, holding hands, saying nothing. What more was there to say? I would always have my paper flowers and my satin heart. And if, someday, they were lost or destroyed, I would still carry them in my mind and in my heart.

Twelve

When we'd arranged the picnic on the blue-and-white cloth beside the river and tethered Fifi to a tree, I told Stefan about my dream.

"I know what you'll say," I said. "And I can't be as skeptical as I was before. It seemed so real. Maybe there is something to Seeing."

"There is," he said.

"And the people in the dream—it's as if I really know them. It's the weirdest thing."

"Not so weird," he said.

I shook my head. "I know what my mother would say."

"She can be wrong," Stefan said. "She's wrong about you."

"What about me?"

"You told me she preferred Molly. That was wrong of her. The Roma would never do this. If parents can't love their child the way it should be loved, the child is sent to another family where it can be loved. Every child must be loved with a whole heart."

Quick tears were in my eyes again. The mother who loved me with her whole heart existed thousands of years ago. Or in my dreams. Or both. I blinked and scratched Fifi's ears. She looked up from the lunch scraps she'd been finishing and climbed into my lap.

Stefan stood. "Now it's time for Fifi's bath. I can do this the hard way, in a basin by the tent, with her splashing all over me. Or the easy way, in the river." He unbuttoned his shirt and pulled it and his shorts off to reveal a swimsuit underneath. He took a towel, a bar of soap, and a brush from the string bag. "You want to help us?"

"But I don't have a bathing suit."

"You don't need one. Come in as you are. It's a hot day, you'll dry before you have to go back."

"Okay." I kicked off my sandals and walked along the riverbank with Stefan and Fifi until we came to a flat, gravelly place where we went in. Fifi squealed with joy as she hit the water.

After she'd been scrubbed clean and towel-dried, Stefan again tied her leash to a tree and let her snooze in the shade on the picnic cloth while we stayed in the water.

We floated on our backs close to the bank, out of the current, our fingers touching, our ears underwater. I felt as if I were tuned to another world, with the ageless sounds of the river in my head.

Finally, our fingertips prune-wrinkled and the rest of us waterlogged, we waded back to the bank. Stefan put on his shirt and sandals and I lay on the grass in the sun, feeling my clothes steam around me as they dried. I wished I could keep the sun from lowering in the sky, from finishing this last day for Stefan and me.

I wondered how I would have spent my last day with

Molly if I'd known it was to be the last. Would I have let her wear my favorite earrings, the ones she'd asked to borrow but that I wanted to wear? Would I have insisted that she go in the car with Mark and me? Would I have stayed by her side the whole evening? Or would I not have changed a thing, letting instead the flame of daily ordinariness burn for as long as it could?

What more could I have done on this last day with Stefan to mark it? Nothing, I decided. Nothing but be fully of the flame.

"I have to go," he said, untying Fifi's leash. "You must come to the circus tonight." He put on his shorts and handed me a pass from his pocket. "Tonight will be special. Many of the people have come every night to see us, so we will thank them with extra music, extra effort, extra brilliance. Maybe I can even get nine rings in the air."

I took the ticket and we walked along the path, more slowly than we had on the other days, stretching out the time. We parted at the lane that led through the fields. Stefan kissed my mouth and my cheeks, and said, "See you tonight." He went off, not looking back.

My clothes weren't quite dry but I returned to the hotel anyway, hoping to get to my room without encountering my parents. No such luck. They were just pulling into the parking area as I walked through it.

"Hannah!" my mother cried. "Look at you! What happened?"

"Nothing happened," I said. "I went in the river to help Stefan wash his piglet, that's all."

"In your clothes?"

"I didn't have a swimsuit. Would you have preferred it if I went in naked?"

"It wouldn't surprise me if you had," she said and, turning away from me, entered the hotel.

"Well," I said to my father.

He touched my arm. "She's tired," he said. "She didn't mean it."

I lifted one shoulder and gave him an opaque look. "How was the sightseeing?"

"Interesting," he said, as glad as I was to leave the subject of my mother. "It's fascinating to imagine the lives of the prehistoric people. So tantalizing and frustrating, not knowing just how they did it."

"Could they . . . could they have had tents inside the *abri*, for more protection from the weather?"

"Very good, Hannah. You'd make a grand anthropologist. In some places there's evidence that that was exactly the case. It makes sense. The weather then was a little cooler and wetter than it is now, depending on just exactly when these places were inhabited. There was a moderate interstadial between the ice ages when it would have been fairly pleasant to live here."

I linked my arm through his. "I have no trouble imagining ancient people living around here," I said.

He smiled sweetly at me. "Maybe you'll follow in my footsteps. We can create a dynasty of anthropologists. Like Margaret Mead and Mary Catherine Bateson."

"Maybe I will." One thing I knew for sure, I didn't want to be a chemist.

"Come on," my father said. "Why don't we go into the bar and have a Coke and plan what we'll do tonight."

"You're not embarrassed to be seen with me?"

"Embarrassed?" He honestly didn't seem to know why he should be, even with me standing before him disheveled and damp. "Certainly not." He put his hand on my elbow and ushered me into the small, dark bar, where we were the only customers.

We sat at a table away from the door, sipping our drinks. "I have to go to the circus again tonight," I blurted. "They're leaving in the morning and I have to be there one more time."

"I see," he said, and I thought he really did. "Well, can you have dinner with us?"

I compared his reaction with the one I would have expected from my mother. Fireworks and scolding, outrage and disappointment, warnings and head-shaking.

"Sure. You want to go, too?"

"I don't know if Mother would enjoy that," he said, "but thank you for the invitation. I'm assuming you have another free ticket."

"You assume correctly."

"Well, you go on. You plan on it. I'll make sure Mother has something else to do, though I can't think what right now. I'll talk to the proprietor. Maybe she'll have an idea. I trust you, you know, and I want you to have a good time. It can't be all beer and skittles, having only your old parents to hang out with."

I knew both of us were thinking of the companion I no longer had.

"What the heck are skittles, anyway?" I asked him.

"It's a game, vaguely related to bowling. When you're a famous anthropologist, you'll know these things." He raised his Coke to me. "Beer and skittles. Drink and play."

"You deserve some beer and skittles, too," I said.

He raised his head. "And I'm going to have them. Hannah, you know it's okay to enjoy yourself again, don't you?"

I looked down into my Coke. I had been enjoying myself. And I was also burdened with guilt at doing so. How could I be so greedy and unfair, having Stefan and Fifi, the circus, the canoe ride, the flowers and the heart-shaped pillow, while Molly had nothing?

As if he'd read my mind, Dad said, "For all we know, Molly's having enough celestial beer and skittles to make our poor little earthly ones look pretty pale."

I'd never thought of that. I'd tried not to think of her at all, afraid I'd imagine her lying cold and still in the dark. It was something else entirely to picture her radiant and laughing, finding pleasures that she wished she could share with me.

I took a great shuddering breath of relief and felt the pressure of stifled tears behind my eyes.

Dad put his hand on mine and we sat that way for a while, our drinks forgotten. Finally he said, "You can talk to her, you know. Tell her what you're doing."

If the Travelers believed that the simple mention of a dead person's name could call her back from the Place of Unborn Souls, that the voice of life was strong enough to do that, why shouldn't I believe that Molly could hear me?

I nodded, not trusting my voice yet, afraid I'd unloose the flood that so frightened me.

"I do," he said. "She knows all about this trip. At least my part of it. I bet she'd like to hear about yours. About Stefan and the circus and all."

"You think so?" I was able to choke out.

"I do," he said.

I cleared my throat. "I've been having these odd dreams. I think they're about her. And about me. They're so real, and yet their meaning seems hidden. But I know they're about loss. And maybe about what's left."

"You should pay attention to your dreams," he said after a moment. "The ones you remember are the ones that have something to tell you. All dreams are you talking to yourself. And you know more than you think you do. Pay attention."

My mother thought dreams were neural static, the products of a tired brain discharging electrical energy, with no meaning. I wondered what her dreams looked like to make her think that.

Dad patted my hand. "Why don't we go upstairs so you can get freshened up before dinner?"

"Good idea." I stood and caught sight of myself in the mirror over the bar. *"Great* idea."

Thirteen

I took a long bath and washed my hair twice, the way it says to do on shampoo bottles. Molly and I thought those instructions were a plot by manufacturers to sell twice as much shampoo. We also thought shampoo was the silliest word in the English language. It sounded like a swear word thought up by a little kid.

I stood by the open French doors, brushing my hair dry and looking down at the river. I'd been in it and on it and seen a stretch of it. But the water I'd been in and on was someplace else now, someplace I'd probably never see. Maybe a nicer place than this, though this was pretty nice.

I put on perfume and a new sundress I hadn't worn yet. *Look, Mol. What do you think? I've got a big date with a Gypsy juggler and his pig. He's breaking my heart.*

There was no answer. Had I thought there would be? Often, before, when I talked to her, she didn't answer. She knew I knew she'd heard me and that was enough. Maybe it could be again.

———

Dad was the star at dinner. He might have been over-acting for my benefit and Mother's, to make it seem that we were having a better time than we actually were, but he was certainly excited.

"Think about this," he was saying. "Think about living in one of those shelters. I could bop anybody I wanted to with my club and drag my woman around by the hair." He patted my mother's hand, and she closed her fingers around his.

"You better not try it," she said, "unless you want to get bopped back."

"Only kidding, Mother," he said. "Likely it wasn't that way at all. Women were probably highly valued and carefully protected. Likely even worshipped. After all, without them there was no future for the race. Even then, the men must have noticed that only women have babies."

"Do you think they knew where the babies came from, Dad? Or did they think women just magically produced them?" It was the kind of question I'd have been embarrassed to ask my mother—Molly and I used to say the words *sex* and *parents* should never be used in the same conversation. But with Dad it was different. Maybe because he was an anthropologist and these questions could be theoretical.

"I don't know. What do you think?"

"I don't see how they could have figured it out," I said. "I didn't believe it when I first heard. I thought it was preposterous. Besides, it's all so invisible. And there're those nine months to wait that would make you doubt any cause-and-effect connection."

Dad nodded judiciously. "Good point. What do you think, Mother?"

"I think they were intuitive and curious or they

wouldn't have survived at all. I think they could have puzzled it out." For the first time in months, she was joining in a conversation with interest. I'd almost forgotten how animated her face could be. "Anyway, surely they noticed that some of the babies looked just like their fathers. How else could they have explained that?"

"Spirits," my father said. "They must have been great believers in spirits, since they could explain so little by science. Why couldn't a man's spirit affect a woman's baby, especially if he cared about her? Don't forget, it's impossible for us to cleanse our minds of modernism enough to imagine how they must have thought."

"Isn't it fascinating to try?" she asked, and her beautiful voice had a particular vibrance to it.

"What a miracle a baby must have been," my father mused. "A new life that a woman created and could feed, all out of her own body."

It occurred to me that this wasn't the most tactful conversation to be having with a woman whose miracle baby was no longer around. But Molly had been my father's child, too, and he chose to remember the miracle as well as the loss.

His eyes were shining and he had an inward look, as if he could see a family around a fire, wearing skins and furs, nursing babies and making tools.

I could see them, too. I *had* seen them. And in my mind's eye, beside those fires, stuck in the ground by their pointed feet, were hearth goddesses made of stone or wood, little statues that glorified the shape and function of woman.

"Think how few people there were," Dad went on. "Actually, there was probably very little bopping with clubs, considering how valuable every single life must have been. And women were the most valuable because they were so vital. Must have felt good to be a woman then.''

My mother opened her mouth. I knew she was about to say something about how it was too bad that attitude hadn't lasted. Or how women should be doubly valued now because they not only did all the same things they'd done then but held jobs, too. It was odd that I agreed with a lot of what she said and still was irritated and offended by the way she said it. She was often so belligerent and fierce it was hard for me to even listen to her. Molly said I paid too much attention to the medium and not enough to the message, and I knew she was right, but I couldn't help it.

My mother shut her mouth and gave a slow shake of her head, as if she were too tired to get into all this again, the same things she'd said too many times already. My shoulders, hunched defensively, relaxed.

I'd finished my dessert. I could leave now for the circus, even if it was way too early. And once I was gone I didn't care if they debated all night about women's place at the hearth fire, or where babies came from.

I put my napkin on the table and stood. "I have to go," I said. "I'll see you later."

Dad took my wrist and held it lightly. "Have a good time, honey. No running away with the circus, now. We need you at home."

"Don't worry," I said. "They wouldn't want me."

"Anybody would," Dad said loyally. Mother kept silent.

I walked out of the dining room, but as soon as I was through the doors I ran—across the lobby, down the front steps, hopping over the cats still lying on the warm stone of the top step, through the parking area and out into the main street, on my way to the path through the fields, to the circus tent, to Stefan.

For tonight, I would pretend that tomorrow and the next day and the next would be the same as the ones that had gone before, having picnics by the river, juggling plums, playing with Fifi. And returning Stefan's kisses.

I wouldn't look at the end until I had to.

Fourteen

I was very early. There were only a few people inside the tent, expectant, while several others wandered outside, letting their children peer at Babette waiting behind the tent in her finery to begin the spectacle.

I went in and sat in my usual seat in the front row. Stefan's circus world was as strange and alluring to me as the ancient one I had seen in my dreams.

By now the opening parade was familiar, and I waited for Stefan to appear, leading Fifi, waving to the children in the crowd. I had to admit, I wondered what he would do this last night to match the flowers and satin hearts of the past two nights.

His clown suit was different this time. He had the same wig and big shoes, the same red nose and stuffed white gloves, but his overalls were covered with red sequins, and Fifi wore a red sequined hat and a bow around her neck. They both glittered when the spotlight hit them. In the spotlight, with Fifi at his feet, Stefan launched a dazzling arc of sequined red balls. They flew so fast they made a merry blur over his head. I thought of his wounded hand and of his determination in spite of it, and hoped that though his trick appeared to use one hundred balls, there were really only nine.

The acts progressed in their usual order, and Stefan's bubbles were as big a success as ever. The horses performed, and then Leoni, Stefan's mother, came on with her trained dogs. While the dogs performed, Babette, huge and patient, waited at the back of the tent, as calm as a diva who knows she's the show's real star.

As the dogs left the ring, leaping over and over through the hoop that Leoni, running, held, Babette heard her music begin and started forward with her bouncy, shuffling gait, oddly graceful and awkward at the same time. She ran around the ring, then stopped, rearing back on her hind legs, her front legs in the air, her trunk raised, turning ponderously so that she faced each of the sides of the tent in turn.

She was sitting on a big stool, facing away from me when Stefan, holding Fifi under his arm, ran across the ring and straight up Babette's back just as she lowered her front legs and stood up, leaving him upright on her back, looking aghast. He held one big white glove against his cheek, his mouth a red O, his eyebrows all the way up at the top of his forehead. He held Fifi out in front of him as if consulting her about what to do. Then he fell onto his stomach and clung to Babette's harness as if for dear life. He must also have been tying Fifi's leash to the harness, for when he began looking for a way down from Babette's broad back as she danced around the ring, Fifi was safely secured.

Babette stopped periodically on her trip around the ring to beg peanuts from the children in the audience.

They were both thrilled to be singled out by her and terrified by her huge head and delicate questing trunk. The wonder on their faces when she daintily took peanuts from their little hands was inexpressible.

Then Babette stopped in front of me. I had no peanuts. I tried to show her that by presenting to her my open, empty hands. She kept her trunk out pleadingly, and then she began to run it over me, as if searching me. In spite of myself, I was frightened. She was so big. What if she thought I was deliberately withholding peanuts from her? What if she had a temper tantrum? I shrank into my seat.

"Stand up!" Stefan called down to me from her back.

I shook my head, withdrawing farther into my seat.

"She won't hurt you," he said. "Stand up."

"Are you sure?"

"Yes. It's okay."

Slowly, I got to my feet.

I smiled for the children who were watching, trying to be an example to them of adult fearlessness and good humor. My stomach felt as if a colony of butterflies had just come out of their cocoons.

With great gentleness, Babette coiled her trunk around my waist and lifted me off my feet. "Oh, my," I said as I rose into the air.

Somehow, between the efforts of Babette and Stefan and my own dazed scramblings, I found myself straddling her, my legs sticking almost straight out over her wide back, my hands clamped onto her harness. The children in the audience screamed, all of them convinced, I was sure, that they would have been braver and more enthusiastic than I.

Fifi squealed with pleasure and got as close to me as

her short leash would allow, evidently wanting her ears scratched. I couldn't let go of the harness long enough to do that. I knew Stefan thought we were safe, but I'd read those stories about the sweet old animals in zoos and circuses who, for reasons of their own, suddenly reverted to their wild ways and threw or clawed or ate unwary keepers and spectators. What was to prevent Babette from turning rogue and tossing me off to be trampled into pudding in the dirt?

Stefan came to sit by me, still looking worried for the benefit of the crowd, but not sounding it at all as he said, "Hi."

"Oh, Stefan, are you out of your mind?"

"You aren't enjoying yourself?" he asked, his voice light. "How many people do you know who can say they've ridden on an elephant? With a pig?"

"Oh, God," I said. "Are you sure this is safe?"

"As safe as your mother's arms."

"Oh, God," I repeated.

"I'd like to kiss you," he said, "but I'd get my makeup all over you."

I forgot about the elephant. "I don't care," I said.

With that, he leaned over and kissed me. Thoroughly. The crowd went nuts. Those French! as my father would say.

Then Stefan fell over on his back so suddenly that I was afraid he was going to slip to the ground. Instead, he held both hands over his heart, thumping one on top of the other, beaming beatifically. I guess he was trying to convey that all it took was the love of a good woman to cure his fear of being on an elephant. The audience seemed to get it. I wondered how much of the noise they were making had to do with the amount of his makeup that must be on my face now.

Strangely, the kiss had cured my fear of elephants, too, and I waved to the audience. Might as well make this something I could tell my grandchildren. And Molly, when I got the chance.

Stefan must have given Babette some sort of signal, or maybe it was the music, but she made one last trip around the ring and then lumbered out through the flap in the back of the tent as a troupe of aerialists rushed in to a different tune from the band.

Now that I wasn't afraid anymore of being on top of Babette, I wasn't ready to get off.

"What now?" I asked Stefan.

"You want to stay aboard and ride her in the finale?"

"Could I? Will you be up here, too?"

"Do you want me?"

"Yes." Our eyes held for a moment before I added, "But I definitely need some plumes."

He laughed. "So now it's plumes. You're more interested in the glamour than the hard work."

I laughed, too. "Always have been. This is a lot more fun than squashing plums."

"I guess I can understand that." He said something to Babette in Romany, and she put up her trunk and helped him down. "I'll be back in a minute with the plumes and a washcloth. You're wearing as much of my clown white as I am."

He brought more than plumes and a washcloth; he brought a whole costume. Red sequins to match his and Fifi's. And a Polaroid camera to take a picture of me after I got down, changed, and remounted Babette. I made it back aboard her just in time to begin the finale.

Stefan rode behind me, his arm around my waist. "My fans will expect it," he said. "They know I'm not the kind of clown to fall in love on the back of an elephant and then desert my lady."

I was still thinking about his words—"fall in love"—when Babette lurched through the tent flap and jogged around the ring to the music of the finale. The spotlight hit us, and I blinked. I couldn't see a thing except light, but I smiled to the people I knew were there, waving and bobbing my plumes, with Fifi nestled in my lap. Stefan rested his head on my shoulder. Babette slowed down with each circuit around the ring, until finally she walked out, her head as high and imperious as royalty.

I changed back into my ordinary clothes behind a stack of hay bales. When I returned, Stefan was getting Babette out of her sequins.

"Babette's got to go to work taking down the tent," he said, unfastening buckles under her stomach. "And so do I."

"You can't go for coffee or anything?" I asked, the disappointment obvious in my voice.

He turned to me. "No. There's too much to do to get ready to go."

I wasn't going to make a scene or do anything stupid and embarrassing like cry. "Okay. Well, it was great meeting you. And Fifi, too. I'll never forget my ride on an elephant. I'd better be getting back to the hotel."

He took me by the arm. "Wait. I don't want to say goodbye like this, but now there's no time. Would you come back before we leave?"

"What? You mean at 3 a.m. or something?"

"No, not then. But at, say, five? Just before we go. I'll be free then." Even as he spoke, one of his cousins passed him, giving him a push on the shoulder and saying something in Romany.

"Okay, okay," Stefan said to him. To me he said, "I have to go. Will you come back?"

How could I not? "Sure. Five o'clock, then."

With that, he turned back to Babette as other members of his family began dismantling the aerialists' net. I wasn't oblivious to the looks many of them gave me as they set to work, though none of them spoke to me. Surely they were remembering the Parisienne who had lured Stefan's brother Karel away from them. What sort of message had Stefan sent them by kissing me in the full glare of the spotlight? What sort of harm had I done him by allowing it?

I started along the path through the fields, the lights from the tent growing dimmer behind me, the darkness of the soft summer night wrapping its scented folds around me.

I walked more slowly as I approached the hotel, reluctant to end the evening, apprehensive about my dreams now that loss was freshly on my mind again. I stood behind the hotel and counted windows, relieved to find the ones in my parents' room dark. My own balcony windows were open, as I left them when I was drying my hair. I felt almost as if I could look in and see myself already in my room, getting ready for bed.

In the past few days I had felt both more like my old self, the way I'd been before Molly died, and more like a total stranger to myself, even stranger than I'd been for the last six months. With Stefan I'd had totally unexpected new experiences, and my odd dreams had given me yet another part of myself to wonder about. Was there really such a thing as the Sight? And if there was, did I have it? I knew my mother thought I had an overactive imagination, and

I probably did, but surely these dreams required more than imagination.

And if the dreams were, as my father thought, only me speaking to myself, what was I telling myself? That loss was nothing new? That people of all times had suffered it? Well, so what? Every loss was unique to the person experiencing it, and the pain of it was real and awful.

I walked around to the front of the hotel. The streets were quiet now, the circus traffic gone, and I could hear the liquid sighing of the river and the song of frogs along the bank. They were loud. It was probably some Frenchman kept awake one long night by an amphibian chorus who wrote the recipe for frog's legs.

I went upstairs to bed, carrying in my hand the Polaroid picture of me wearing red sequins, safe atop an elephant.

Fifteen

The cave called to her, called through her fear, through her efforts to ignore it, through her sleep. When she ground the manganese and the ochers and iron oxide, when she mixed them with deer fat and blood, when she formed them into crayons, her fingers ached to draw on the calcite walls of the cave, the white surfaces sparkling like sunlight on new snow. But that was part of her old life, a life that was finished, and she couldn't go back.

She could forget about it only in the river with Mai, drifting naked in the cool current, the sun hot on her scars. These summer days were precious, the last ones they would spend as sisters before Mai, who would be married right after the woman ceremony, left the summer grounds to go to her new family's winter home. They floated on their backs, their hair spread weightless around their heads, their fingers touching, bouyant and tender, until the current took Mai and pulled her away.

Adrift. Aware of the hot sun above her and the cool, round river stones below her. The round stones that were so good for grinding pigments.

She stood at the cave's entrance, the hot smell of pines around her, her breath coming fast. Inside, it was cool and beautiful and sacred. She wanted to be there, feeling the power of the animal spirits, sensing their movement in the flickering light of the fat lamps. But she was so afraid. She was different now. Changed forever. How could she go back to what she had known before? How could she enter a cave again?

Then, somehow, she was in the narrow passage, in the dark, her heart thudding. She thought she could also hear the slow, strong beat of Earth-the-Mother's huge heart, guiding her. Mai wasn't an artist, didn't enter the caves except for the ceremonies, but it was Mai she wanted with her now, Mai, whose hand she had always reached for in troubles. Mai, who had been by her side every day of her life. Yet her feet moved her forward, alone, until she heard voices echoing off stone, saw the waver of flame, the flush of life it gave to the shimmering walls.

Mother saw her and came, her hands outstretched. "I knew you'd find us," she said. "I knew you'd come back. What will you draw?"

An-Nay understood that it should be an important animal, a big one. The smaller animals, and the fish, of course, had their own qualities, but they weren't substantial enough, significant enough to inspire the boys to become what they needed to be.

"A bird," she said, to her surprise. "I want to draw a bird."

Mother frowned. "A bird?" Then her face cleared. "If that is what you're moved to draw, then you must draw it. It's unusual, but there is a reason for it, even if we can't know what it is." Then Mother was gone.

She faced the perfect white wall. An animal had to be captured in the mind first, and then put on the wall on the first try, to contain all his power.

Birds were strong. They tended their children well. They traveled far—and what could be more wonderful than to fly? How could a bird not be as worthy as a bison?

She made swift strokes with her black crayon and the bird came to life before her, soaring, taking her up with it, her heart lifting with the joy of regaining a part of herself she'd thought gone forever.

After the bird, other images flew from her crayon and from the macerated end of a hornbeam branch onto the irregular, glittering surface of the cave walls in a way they never had before. A reddish wash on the flank of a deer appeared to turn to muscle before her eyes. The brown shoulder of a bison flexed and stretched upon the wall.

The life she had had to give up seemed somehow to have transformed itself into the life of her art. She returned often to the cave, working in a fever of creative energy. Sometimes she worked alone, sometimes with others, but always at one with her animal spirits—strength, serenity, wisdom, guile.

When she wasn't in the cave, she and Mai floated in the river, swung apart and together by the capricious currents, sensitive always to the nearness of the other.

When it was time for the woman ceremony, they stood in the circle of women, together, joined by their hands and their hearts, their histories and their uncertain futures. Together they received from Mother their hearth goddesses, big of breast and belly and hip, with pointed feet to be plunged into the earth beside their own hearth fires. However far apart they might be, the same goddess would watch over them both until the stone she was made of became dust.

Before the tears in her eyes had dried, still hand in hand with Mai, she followed the boys and their families to the cave.

Light from the fat lamps shifted and moved on the walls, and moved the animals with it. Alone with them, she had seen the animals being playful or carefree, but now, as if they understood the great duty they had, to teach the boys the important lessons of manhood, they stood silent: grave, noble, and potent.

After the involuntary in-drawing of breath that everyone always made on first seeing the paintings, the hunters began their chanting. The sounds echoed in the rock chamber, the bosom of Earth-the-Mother, in a lulling, hypnotic rhythm.

Each boy was called forward, in the light of a single torch, to be consecrated in his new role, reminded of his obligations to Earth-the-Mother and to the life-carrying women who were her daughters.

She waited outside the cave then, with the other women, for the conclusion of the ceremonies, the private rites that only men could witness. The scent of hot vegetation was in the air, and the late-summer sun rested on her shoulders. Somehow its rays felt false, a kind of trick, with cold lying barely behind them, the foretoken of winter. Oh, how she hated winter.

She must try to remember that spring always came again, the gift of Earth-the-Mother for enduring the cold time. And even in winter there were pleasures: the family together in the shelter, the fire, the taste of summer in the dried meat and berries. Except that next winter—and all the winters after— Mai would be gone. Perhaps they would be together in the summers, but there could be no promise of that. Life was perilous and uncertain.

When the time came for the boys and their families to place their handprints on the cave walls, she and Mai hung back, waiting to be last. They watched the others blow the powdered pigment onto the damp wall, leaving the stenciled outlines of their hands, recording their presence at the ceremony.

Finally, they made their own handprints, a bit apart from the others, overlapping, touching for endless time.

Sixteen

The alarm sounded and I was sitting up before my eyes were open, my heart thudding. Four o'clock. I was still caught in my dream, wishing in some buried part of me that I could have what An-Nay had—her devotion to Mai, to her art, to things outside herself that filled her life and gave it meaning in spite of what she had lost because of her scars.

I swung my legs to the side of the bed and sat for a minute, catching my breath. Of course An-Nay and Mai were figments of my imagination. I stood, swayed, and straightened. Quickly I dressed, taking a bit of extra time to put on a drop of perfume, a bit of lip gloss, a flick of mascara. I wanted my last image in Stefan's mind to be a good one. I wrote my address on a slip of paper and put it into my jeans pocket. I'd decide when I saw him if I wanted to give it to him.

I closed my door quietly and stole down the stairs. The hotel's front doors were unlocked, and I stepped outside into the soft darkness of the early-summer morning. The cats were prowling; I could see their yellow eyes peering at me from the profusion of geraniums at the edges of the parking area, and I heard them rustle among the leaves. I made a little kissing sound in their direction, a sound of sisterhood and solidarity—I was a prowler in the dark, too.

There were only a few lights on in the village. Someone up with a sick child? A good book? A clandestine meeting, like mine?

I made my way along the lane through the pastures, considering that I'd never have walked any street in Los Angeles at four-thirty in the morning. There were no lights ahead of me, as there were on nights when the circus was performing. There was no sound, either. Were they gone already? Had they finished packing and left earlier than they expected?

I hurried along, dreading what I might find. I held my breath until I saw the indistinct humps of the motor homes and trucks that housed the dismantled circus and its performers. They must all be catching catnaps before moving on.

I stopped beside the motor home I'd seen Stefan come out of on the day of one of our picnics. Maybe he'd forgotten I was coming. Maybe he was in there asleep, thinking only about the next performance and not about me.

I was ready to turn around and go back to the hotel before anyone discovered me, before I embarrassed myself, when I heard a whisper. "Hannah?"

"Where are you?"

Stefan came out from behind the motor home.

Suddenly I was shy. We should have said goodbye earlier. What point was there in dragging this out? Nothing had changed. He was going now as surely as he had been earlier. "Where's Fifi?" I asked.

I saw his wide shoulders move under his sweatshirt in a shrug. "Sleeping. She's just a baby, you know."

We stood silently looking at each other, barely discernible in the dimness. Finally I said, "Don't you have a saying for this situation?"

I heard what might have been a laugh. "I can't think of one. But give me time."

We were silent again. I couldn't stand it. "I don't know what to say," I said. "Goodbyes aren't my favorite thing. I shouldn't have come."

"Yes, you should. Goodbyes are important."

"Why? You know and I know that you're leaving. Isn't that enough?"

"You're afraid to feel sad. Why are you so afraid of that?"

"Isn't everybody?" I asked. "Who wants to feel bad?"

"Does ignoring your feelings make it any better?" he asked.

I raised my voice. "I'm sad already. I don't need more."

"It's like a wound," he said, unconsciously raising his hand, the one with the open cut. "It has to be cleaned to heal. Feeling your sadness is the cleansing. Tears wash the wound." He paused. "I'm sad." There was a tremor in his voice. "I would like to know you better, to see what happens between us. I have a feeling it would be very good. But we don't always get what we want."

"No kidding," I said bitterly.

"Think of all the time ahead. We can't know what our futures hold."

"Mine seems to hold nothing but goodbyes."

He came closer to me and put his arms around me. I held myself away from him, but he pulled me against him. Sighing, I put my head on his chest and squeezed my eyes shut to stem the tears. Tears wouldn't help my wounds. They were as permanent as An-Nay's scars.

"Someday," he whispered to me. "Who can know?"

I shook my head against him. "Don't give me hope. It makes disappointment harder."

"Then just remember," he said. "I will."

"It's not enough."

"No," he said. "But it's something. It's a way I can be with you forever. And you with me. Remember the plums, the bubbles, Fifi, Babette—all the little things. That's what makes a life, the little things. It gives one a lot to remember. How much we have from our few days."

"I want more." This was the same asking song I always sang. I hadn't had enough. I wanted more.

His chest lifted and lowered in a great breath. "But this is what we have."

I raised my head. "You're going to leave the circus, aren't you? You're going to your brother in Paris. When?"

"I don't know. I don't know if I can leave at all, no matter how much I miss him or how restless I am. The circus has been my life. But I must trust my instincts, make my own path, even if the way is rough. And if I do leave, I'll go to Karel, of course."

I took the slip of paper with my address on it from my pocket. "Here. It's my address. But don't write to me unless you leave the circus. There's nothing ahead for us unless you do. There's probably nothing ahead for us, anyway."

He took the paper from me, and in the changing light of coming dawn I could see him smile. "An optimistic pessimist. Thinking of future possibilities, even if you don't want to."

A light went on in one of the trailers and Stefan turned his head to it, then back to me. "We're going soon."

"Okay," I said.

He bent his head and kissed me. Of all the times I'd wanted a running clock to stop, this was when I wanted it most.

When he raised his head I asked him, "What about that kiss on top of Babette? What does your family think about that?"

"They probably aren't thrilled, but no one's said anything. If they ask, I'll tell them it was just show business." He kissed me again. "But it wasn't."

He gave me a last embrace and released me. "I thought of a saying," he said.

"What?" I didn't trust myself to say anything more.

"It's something we often say at funerals—when there is no choice but to say goodbye. *Akana mukav tut le Devlesa.* I leave you now to God."

"And you," I whispered. And turned and ran.

By the time I got back to the hotel, it was barely light, and my jaws and throat and head ached from the effort of holding back tears. I could hear the sounds of voices and crockery from the kitchen, but no one was in the lobby. I raced up the stairs to my room and locked myself in.

The pain of loss was physical. I could feel it in my stomach and behind my eyes, along every nerve. I felt afire and frozen at the same time, the way I had for weeks after Molly, until the ice solidified and covered me. I didn't want to have to feel anything ever again. I didn't want this whistling emptiness, this terror. Why couldn't I stay cold and numb and remote? Love was such an awful mistake. It only opened the door to loss.

I covered my ears with my hands to block my own dry, anguished sounds. I wouldn't cry. I wouldn't.

I couldn't sleep again. I wasn't hungry for breakfast. I didn't want to go sightseeing. I didn't even want to talk to anyone. All I wanted was to be left alone. My excuse of a headache seemed lame, even though it was the truth, but my father accepted it generously, without question. He took my mother off to Market Day in Sarlat to look at the medieval architecture and the pâtés, truffles, and walnut products for sale.

I sat at the river's edge where Stefan and I had bathed Fifi, watching the sunlight fall through the poplars in golden coins that dappled the grass and dropped, sparkling, into the water.

I dangled my bare feet in the water and wondered how long it would take me to learn to spear a fish. When my feet became shriveled from being so long in the water, I pulled them out and lay back on the warm grass, covering my face with the bandana from around my neck. It was easy to believe that, if I stayed quiet long enough, an aurochs would come for the sweet water and grass. I smiled when I thought of what Molly could do with that: Hottest Gourmet Dining Spots for Wild Game. Places with the Freshest Produce and Finest Spa Waters. Uncrowded. Ambiance to Die For.

To Die For.

Tears rose behind my closed eyes. I squeezed my lids

tight, but the tears pressed and swelled and grew until I couldn't keep them in. At first they oozed slowly, wetting my lashes. But I could feel the pressure of them building until it seemed as if my entire body was filled with tears, my skin a fragile barrier to them, ready to rupture if there wasn't some release.

I'd spent so much energy damming up those tears and denying them. Finally I was exhausted from the effort, and helpless besides. I opened my eyes and the tears poured out, running down the sides of my face, backing up in my throat until I had to turn on my side to keep from choking. The sounds I made, the sobs, were so loud and strangled that they scared me—and certainly would have frightened away any aurochs in the vicinity.

Unexpectedly, once that noisy storm was over—and it was not soon—I felt better. Well, maybe not better, since my nose was stopped up, my eyes were swollen, and my throat was sore, but different. Different in a better way, as if I'd gone around a corner and the landscape there wasn't so bleak; as if the hard cold thing inside me had thawed a bit and the pressure in my chest had eased. Apparently horrible, filthy grief wasn't fatal. Like a fire—or a lion attack—it was something that could be survived, albeit with scars.

Curled on my side, the soggy bandana in my hand, thinking of Molly's Restaurant Review for Extinct Species, which I knew wasn't really Molly's but mine, or Molly going on, somehow, in me, I fell asleep.

Seventeen

I woke with a start. I lay in the grass, still holding the bandana, my eyes puffy and my nose stuffed. The sun was several degrees closer to the horizon, and I knew I'd slept for quite a while, a restful, dreamless sleep.

Molly seemed near. The nearest I'd felt her since she died.

Died.

I could say it now, and know what it meant. She was gone, gone for good. But not really. She was in my mind and in my heart. As long as she stayed there, she'd never be completely gone. I felt as if I could almost touch her.

And I knew with certainty that I was going to have a different life now, without her, one I'd better start getting used to.

When I sat up, my sinuses cleared some. Good old gravity. At the river's edge, I dipped my bandana into the cold water and held it against my swollen eyes.

I didn't know how I would spend the rest of the afternoon. All I knew was that I didn't want to go back to the hotel—not yet. So I wandered. I sat by the river. I watched the birds and the changing light and the trees stirring sluggishly in the hot summer breeze. I listened to the buzz of insects and the movement of water over rocks and the rustle of leaves. Time seemed elastic, stretching out forever, leisurely and at the same time rushing along, speeding away from memories I wanted to hold on to. I could already sense those memories dimming, the way a dream does when you wake. But the feelings that went with the memories remained. The heart remembers better than the brain.

I spoke to Molly, told her of my dreams and of my waking life. And while I talked, the air around me quieted, as if listening. Now that my healing had begun, maybe I could listen to myself, maybe I could find my own future, the way An-Nay found hers. The way Stefan would find his.

I once had friends and things I liked to do. Perhaps they were waiting for me to come back to them. If not, or if I had changed too much to fit back into my previous life, there would be new friends to make, new projects to begin.

Finally, when the sun was low behind the trees, I started back to the hotel. My father would be frantic and my mother might even have noticed I was gone.

I was walking along the road, listening to the frogs sing in the weeds by the river, when a car with its headlights on pulled to a stop beside me. I stepped back before I recognized our rented Citroën with my father behind the wheel. He opened his door and got out, calling to me over the roof of the car.

"Hannah? Are you all right?" His voice had that tone of a worried person trying not to sound worried.

"I'm fine," I said. "I wouldn't mind a ride, either." I opened the car door and got in on the passenger side.

My father got in, too, and made a U-turn, not without difficulty on that narrow road. "Are you hungry?" he asked.

I hadn't noticed before, but once he mentioned it, my empty stomach responded with a roar. "Does that answer your question?" I asked, and we both laughed.

We rode in silence the rest of the way to the hotel. As he parked the car, I said, "I'd like to have dinner in my room tonight."

"Any special reason?" he asked, ever tactful.

"I just want to think and be quiet. These restaurant meals seem too festive when I'm not feeling that way. You know what I mean?"

"Putting on a happy face can be a drag, can't it?"

I rested my head on his shoulder. People were a mystery. He and I were such a good match; my mother and I such a poor one—and yet the two of them seemed to do well together, even though I'd never understand it. It was true that she and Molly were a good match, too. But not as good as Molly and I were.

My eyes filled—part love, part grief, part weariness. Since I'd broken the dam of my tears, it seemed I could breathe more easily, but all my emotions were easier to reach, too.

"Yeah," I said to Dad. "Yeah."

"Okay, honey." He squeezed my hand. "Mother—Anne—and I'll have some *vin* and get rowdy without you around to keep us in line."

"Do you good," I said.

"It would at that."

We separated at our respective rooms and I closed the

door behind me with gratitude. Twilight shadows were pooled, purple and charcoal, in the corners, though the window still held the day's last pink-and-silver gleam. I wondered about the color of the light where Molly was now. And Stefan.

I didn't turn on a lamp until my dinner arrived, and then only a small one. I put the tray outside my door when I finished, and turned off the lamp again. The window was open to the velvet night. I undressed in the dark, though it wasn't really dark. Some light filtered up from the dining-room windows below my room, and other light seemed to come from the night itself, the way the cave in my dream had produced its own light.

I lay in bed, nestled in the night, remembering Molly and Stefan.

Eighteen

I woke to find my father sitting on the side of my bed.

"Hey, sleepyhead," he said. "These French hours are getting away from us. We leave this afternoon for the Midi."

I yawned and stretched and pushed up onto my elbows. "Okay, I'm pretending to be awake. What do you want to do with these French hours?"

"Why don't we go look for our own painted cave? They're supposed to be all around here, just waiting to be discovered. If a dog could find Lascaux, why can't we find one?"

"No problem," I said, running my fingers through my hair. "Heck, we've got until afternoon. We can probably find a couple of them by then."

My father laughed. "Okay, okay. We'll bring a lunch and binoculars to see the birds, and we'll take a hike. The three of us."

I blinked. "Are you going to make Mom go, too?"

"She wants to go." He interpreted the look on my face. "Really."

"Right. Well, sure, fine. I'll get dressed."

When I came out of the shower, there was a cup of cocoa and a croissant on the bureau. I worked on them as I dressed. I was brushing my hair in front of the mirror when my mother opened the door between our rooms without knocking. In the mirror, I saw myself frown before I turned to her. She saw it, too.

"I'm sorry," she said hastily. "I should have knocked. That was thoughtless." Thoughtless or not, she stayed, closing the door and leaning back against it, one hand behind her on the knob, as if anticipating a quick getaway.

I turned back to the mirror and kept brushing my hair, even though it no longer needed it.

"Hannah."

I looked at her through the chill medium of the mirror.

"Hannah," she said again, and made a vague gesture with her hand. She sighed. "I haven't been much help to you. I suppose I don't blame you for being angry with me." Her musical voice made the words sound sincere.

"Yes?" I said, wondering what the punch line was going to be.

My mother sighed again. "This . . . with Molly . . . has been hard on all of us."

I was silent.

"You're my only child now."

I stopped brushing, but continued to look at her through the mirror.

"You're not making this easy for me, you know," my mother said, a familiar tautness in her melodious voice. Molly might have been able to ignore that tone, or laugh it away, but I couldn't.

And just what was it that I was supposed to be making easy for her? She'd practically ignored me since Molly died. What did she want to say now?

My mother closed her eyes and put one hand on her stomach, as if she felt sick. When she opened her eyes, they were full of tears.

I turned to face her. "I miss her, too, you know. She was half of me. I'm always going to be alone now." I blinked to keep my own tears back. "I know that because I look like her I remind you all the time of what you've lost. I suppose that's why you've hardly looked at me since she died." I couldn't trust my voice, so I stopped.

"Oh, Hannah," she whispered, still holding her stomach with one hand and the doorknob with the other.

She can make even a whisper sound like music, I thought.

"It's just that I knew better how to be with Molly," she said. "Because she was more like me. You're so different, so . . . reckless, so unrestrained, so . . . so turbulent. I didn't know what to do with a child who looked at me with that fierce, measuring gaze of yours. As if you were always weighing me, always finding me wanting." She smiled a half smile. "I guess you were."

I didn't know what to say. If I seemed to find her wanting, it was because I thought she'd been disappointed in me. I wanted to hear her say that I was fine, that she liked my turbulence, found it interesting and exciting, that Molly wasn't the only one who was wonderful.

But she didn't say that. She couldn't, I suppose, but she hurt me in a way I'd thought impossible for her to do—not by any deliberate cruelty, but by an honest lack of enthusiasm for who I was. At least, that was the way it seemed to me.

After a long silence she took a deep breath and looked up. "It's true I loved Molly—" Her eyes filled again and she paused. I could see her willing the tears back. I knew how to do that, too. What a pathetic strength we shared, this ability to force back tears. She went on. "But I love you, too. We'll always miss Molly, both of us. But is it really too late for you and me?"

I didn't know how to answer such a question. Too late for what? What did she want? What was I supposed to be for her now that Molly, the buffer between us, was gone?

"I—I don't know," I finally said. Why couldn't she see that I needed help to understand what she wanted, some clue as to how things should be with us now? Why couldn't she read me, the way she would have read Molly, and give me what I needed?

She nodded. "Okay," she said, as if I'd said something final. "Okay." She turned the doorknob behind her, pushed open the door into her room, and backed through it. The door closed with a quiet click.

I sighed. Coming over and giving me a hug never even entered her mind. I knew I'd never refer to this conversation again, and I doubted that she would, so where we were now, at this impasse, was where we would stay.

I sat in the cabbage-rose-upholstered chair to buckle my sandals. So now she wouldn't want to come. It would be just me and Dad bird-watching together this morning. Just as well. We'd have more fun without her.

I stuck a pencil flashlight in my pocket in case we really did go into a cave, and knocked on the door to my parents' room. Without opening it, I called, "I'll meet you downstairs."

I sat in one of the armchairs by the front windows, waiting. Footsteps on the stairs announced my father's arrival, and I stood. Behind him, in walking shoes and a wide-brimmed hat, came my mother. The hat brim shaded her face so that I couldn't see her expression.

"Ah," my father said, a bit too brightly to be natural, "you're here. Let me pick up the picnic I had Madame Lenoir prepare for us and we can go."

With my father gone to the kitchen, my mother and I looked silently away from each other. When my father returned with a basket covered with an embroidered tea towel, I bolted through the front door, not waiting for my parents. I threw myself into the backseat of the Citroën.

Nineteen

I was in no mood to spend the whole morning walking on eggshells around my mother, wondering if I was doing something she found too reckless or too turbulent. Why couldn't she spend one more day in bed so Dad and I could have a last pleasant time together? Hadn't she noticed that the circus was gone? Didn't she make any connection between that and my absence yesterday?

My parents got into the car and no one spoke as we pulled out of the parking area.

"Madame Lenoir told me of a nice place to picnic," my father said finally. "She said there are lots of birds and no tourists and there might even be a cave or two. It's on a bluff overlooking the river. Sounds pretty."

I grunted.

My mother said, "It sounds very nice. It's been too long since I've gone on a picnic."

"That's why we're here," my father said, taking one hand off the wheel to pat her knee. "For you to do some things you ought to be doing more of."

"I know," she said quietly.

We drove along the river, my father pointing out sights and my mother responding with real comments, as if she was actually paying attention. I was silent.

We parked in a gravel area off the road at the foot of a narrow, weedy path that zigzagged to the top of the bluff.

"That's a long way to carry a picnic basket," my mother said.

"We'll take turns," my father said.

The climb was strenuous, and I was sweating by the time we got to the top. I'd hoped the effort would discourage my mother, make her turn around and wait for us in the car. I liked the image of my mother, hot and bored, sitting in the car while Dad and I had a nice hike and a pretty French *pique-nique*. But my mother had forged on, panting and red-faced.

She stood at the top of the path. "I made it," she said, and smiled triumphantly. She held up her hand and Dad gave her a high five. Then she held her hand to me. I hesitated and then tapped my hand lightly against hers. I tried to remember the last time she touched me, and couldn't.

I led the way through the brush, following an overgrown path between bushes that in some places almost met. The trees, as Mme Lenoir had advertised, were full of birds singing their heads off. Even the sounds of us crashing along didn't seem to worry them.

"Dad, do birds sing because they're happy or because they're programmed that way and they can't help it?" I asked, looking over my shoulder at my father.

"Well—" he began, but my mother interrupted.

"That's the kind of question you used to ask when

you were little," she said. "I was usually totally confounded. I could never decide if I should give you the straight, factual answer, or some kid-friendly approximation."

"I remember," I said, stopping and turning around. "You must have done something in-between because I never understood your answers. Dad's I could understand even if they didn't make any scientific sense. He told me that the sky was blue to match my eyes. And that water was wet so little girls could play in it. And that Mopsy purred because cats like to keep themselves company."

There was a silence in which the birdsong began to sound like a competition. My father looked from me to my mother and said nothing.

Finally, my mother spoke. "I guess my question-answering instincts weren't very good. Being a mother wasn't always the easiest thing for me."

"Being a kid wasn't always easy for me," I said. But having Molly there had made it better.

She gave a little laugh. "Maybe we should have helped each other out more."

I couldn't think of a single way I could have helped her. With her Superwoman disposition, it had never even occurred to me that she needed any help.

"Maybe," I said. There was too much behind us that hadn't worked to begin trying to fix it now. It was easier just to go on as we had. Yet the thought of that made me inexpressibly sad.

I sighed and started walking again.

We walked in silence, except for the birds. At a break in the bushes I decided to leave the path. I needed to be alone.

"I'm going to see what's over there," I said. "You don't have to come with me."

And I started off quickly, before anyone could speak or try to stop me.

"We'll wait for you here," my father called. "Don't be long."

I went deeper and deeper into underbrush that, with the sun on it, had a spicy-dusty scent, the hot smell of summer. Away from the path, the brush grew higher, almost as high as my head, but it seemed as if a way opened to me as I walked.

The chestnut trees cast shadows that winked in and out of light, dazzling me, confusing my vision as I traveled through currents of light and shade, warmth and coolness. The bushes became thicker and the passage more difficult. Still I pressed ahead, until a clearing opened before me—and across it, the cool, dark mouth of a cave.

It wasn't the undiscovered cave my father and I had hoped to find. I knew that from the plastic bags caught in the roots of the bushes, the old soft-drink can on the ground. But its secrets drew me nonetheless.

I stepped into the clearing, where the sunlight was strong and pure. The breath of the cave touched my bare arms, a damp, cool contact. I moved closer to the opening, wishing that I would find inside it the place of my dreams. A place where two sets of handprints overlapped on the wall, where strong animal spirits reminded me to be my best self—and reminded me that that self could be loved.

In the beam of my flashlight, the inside of the cave was shallow—no vast, awesome chamber inviting ceremonies. It was also musty and dank, with the smell of rotting vegetation. There was a dirty sock on the ground, and a litter of cigarette stubs.

As I came back out into the sunlit clearing, I heard a crashing in the brush, as if a big animal was making a path. I looked around for a rock or a stick to use as a weapon, but before I could find one, through the bushes and into the clearing came my mother, sweating and out of breath. She had a scratch on her cheek and dirt on her blouse.

"Oh, Hannah," she said. "Thank goodness I found you. I was afraid I'd gotten lost and would bash around out there forever."

"Where's Dad?" I asked, looking behind her. "I thought you were going to wait for me."

"He's waiting for both of us. I wanted to come after you."

"You did?" I said. "Why?"

She fanned herself with her hat. "Want some water?" she asked, holding out a plastic bottle of mineral water.

"Okay," I said, taking it from her. I had a swig and handed it back. She swallowed about half of what was left in the bottle before saying, "Is there somewhere we can sit?"

I pointed to a jumble of rocks by the cave entrance. "That's all there is," I said.

"Will you sit?" she asked.

I shrugged and picked a rock. She sat, still fanning herself.

I waited.

She cleared her throat. "Well, I thought—I mean, this morning, between us, I didn't think that went very well. Did you?"

"I guess I don't know how it was supposed to go."

"Well, that's right," she said. "Of course not. You hadn't been thinking about it the way I had, wondering how to get it right." She gave me a wry look. "Planning how it would work out."

"No," I said. "I hadn't."

"Well, what I thought—I mean, what I realized after, later, is that I may not have made myself clear. I mean, considering how different you and I are." She paused.

"Has Dad been talking to you?" I asked, wondering if my father was behind this effort. If he was, I was really going to be mad at him.

"About you and me? Oh, no, no. He would never . . . but you make a good point."

I wondered what point I'd made.

"I mean, he and I are very different, too, and that seems to work out all right. I think," she went on, "that you and I are used to having Molly between us and we don't know how to be with each other alone."

I waited.

"I, uh, I think, for one thing—Hannah, I wonder if you know how hard this is for me. How hard it is for me to say I don't understand something, that I don't know how to make it right. In chemistry there are formulas that work every time, no surprises. That's probably why I'm a chemist. With people—" She lifted her shoulders. "Who can ever tell?"

"To me," I said, "that's the interesting part."

"Yes," she said. "Well, I might not, I mean, maybe I could have been more understanding about your Gyp— your young man in the circus."

"Stefan," I said.

"Stefan, yes. I know you're lonely. He was a pleasant companion for you and I'll admit I overreacted. But, you know, none of us has been completely sound these last few months."

"And maybe we'll never be completely sound ever again," I said. "I know I'm never going to be exactly the same as I was before."

"Nor I," she said. And then, more softly, "Nor I."

We looked at each other and for the first time the enormous loss we'd suffered was shared between us.

She swallowed. "That's why I thought that now, while everything's still so unsettled, we could, you and I, try to get on a new footing before we slump back down into some bad habits."

"Like what kind of new footing?" I asked, finally able to form a question, trying to pay more attention to the message than to the medium, as Molly said I should.

"Like, maybe, friends?" She was quiet, and when I didn't say anything, she added, "You're my only child now." Her voice wavered. "My only baby."

I was afraid my own voice would betray me. While I struggled with it, before I could speak again, she said, "You know, turbulence can also mean exhilaration, excitement, stimulation. Who wouldn't like to be around someone so interesting?"

A sob escaped me, and I put my hand over my mouth.

She got off her rock and came to me, putting her arms around me, pressing my head against her.

"Oh, baby," she said. "Don't cry."

But she was crying, too.

"Shall we try?" she asked. "And see what happens? You never know. It might be fine."

She was right. The future holds its mysteries.